Carrie picked a p... **S0-ALK-678**

A jagged streak of lightning struck the ground nearby and a deafening clap of thunder ricocheted across the prairie. A wild scream tore from the bay. Beside herself with fear, she reared on her hind legs pawing the air, then jumped to the side, dragging the frightened girl and rocking buggy straight toward a deep gully. Carrie squeezed her eyes shut and hung on for dear life. When she opened her eyes, she saw a tall man on a big black horse riding out of the storm.

He raced past the out-of-control buggy. Then, his gloved hand reached out and grabbed the bridle, turning the bay away from the edge of the gully, and bringing her to a trembling stop.

He looked back at Carrie. "Are you all right, Miss?"

"I am now." She watched as he dismounted. He was tall and broad shouldered. A pearl-handled Colt 45 Peacemaker in a black holster was tied low on his right hip.

As he began to stroke the bay's nose and whisper soothingly to her, Carrie climbed from the buggy. He looked at her and his blue eyes lit up. "I'd say you're more than all right." He grinned.

M. J. CONNER is the pen name for the author team of sisters Mildred Colvin and Jean Norval from Missouri. Mildred is the mother of three—plus a granddaughter—and she and her husband are currently fostering six other children in their home. Jean and her husband are also parents of three and have seven grandchildren. Mildred has published some short stories for children, but this is the first work of adult fiction either author has sold.

Circle
of Vengeance

M. J. Conner

Heartsong Presents

Dedicated to Lester Conner.

"Blessed is the man that walketh not in the counsel of the ungodly, nor standeth in the way of sinners, nor sitteth in the seat of the scornful. But, his delight is in the law of the Lord; and in his law doth he meditate day and night." Psalms 1:1–2
Thank you, Daddy, for daily allowing us to see God in your life. We love you more than can be expressed in these few brief paragraphs. It would take volumes.

Jean and Millie

A note from the author:
I love to hear from my readers! You may correspond with me by writing: **M. J. Conner**
Author Relations
PO Box 719
Uhrichsville, OH 44683

ISBN 1-58660-318-3

CIRCLE OF VENGEANCE

All Scripture quotations, unless otherwise noted, are taken from the King James Version of the Bible.

All of the characters and events in this book are fictitious. Any resemblance to actual persons, living or dead, or to actual events is purely coincidental.

Cover design by Robyn Martins.

PRINTED IN THE U.S.A.

prologue

Western Kansas, 1880

The sharp report of gunfire filled the night as the boy knelt on the floor beside the lifeless body of his mother. The man crouched at the window, the old Henry he'd taken from a dead Union soldier at Shiloh clutched tightly in his hands.

He returned their fire as best he could, but they both knew—the man and his twelve-year-old son—that his effort was hopeless. There were too many of them.

A blazing torch arced through the darkness and landed with a soft thud on the roof, igniting the dry shingles.

The man left his post at the window to kneel beside the woman. He unfastened a locket from around her neck, then gently removed the wedding ring from her finger. He slipped the ring onto the heavy gold chain, then reached across the body of his wife, and clasped the locket around the boy's neck.

His big, rough hand rested for a brief moment against the soft velvet of the boy's face. "Lucas, I want you to climb out the back window."

Wordlessly the boy shook his head.

"Yes, Son! You must. I'm goin' out the door. While I draw their fire I want you to run."

"But, Pa! I can't. I can't leave you."

5

"You must, Son." The man's voice came out harsh with emotion as he struggled to his feet.

A shower of sparks fell around them as the boy leaned down to kiss his mother's pale cheek. Then, his father half carried, half pulled him to the window. He caught him close in a desperate final hug before lifting him onto the sill of the open window.

"As soon as I open the door I want you to run. Run, Lucas, and don't look back. Don't never look back. And, always remember—vengeance belongs to the Lord."

"You comin' out, Reb, or you gonna stay in there and fry." The disembodied voice came from the darkness in front of the house and cut off anything else the father might have said to his son.

Darting around the small fires that had flared up, the man burst through the door. A barrage of gunfire sent him sprawling backward into the burning room.

The boy hesitated for only a moment before dropping to the ground. He ran, darting from one shadowy spot to the next.

He didn't stop to look back until he reached the deep shadows. The flickering flames revealed a half-dozen men standing together, watching the burning house. He didn't recognize any of them.

While the boy watched, the roof fell in, sending up an illuminating flare of light. In the shadows cast by the big tree, behind and to one side of the huddled men, the boy caught a glimpse of a man on horseback. Then, the fire died down and the cover of darkness concealed the man once more.

The boy knew that man. There was no mistaking him. His broad-shouldered height and the tall bay horse he rode set him apart. He'd been harassing them ever since their family came here from Tennessee a year ago. Cutting their fences. Running off their cows. Muddying their water hole.

Hatred for the big man welled in the boy's heaving chest. His hands clenched at his sides, as the desire for revenge became a living thing inside him.

"Someday I'll be a man," he whispered through clenched teeth. "And when I'm strong enough, I'll come back. Someday you'll pay for what you've done."

A wall crashed into the blazing inferno. Once more the flames leapt high, illuminating the big man and briefly revealing the umber silhouettes of several mounted figures behind him.

The man turned his head toward the boy's hiding place. In the brief moment before the fire died back down, the boy memorized the big man's face. Then, choking back sobs, he turned and ran into the darkness.

one

Western Kansas, 1892

Despite the gloomy sky overhead, Carrie whistled softly as she prepared to leave the ranch house. Fearing the coming storm, Papa had been reluctant to let her go. He gave his permission grudgingly, only after she explained to him the importance of this trip to town. She promised him she would hurry and assured him that Gretchen would be with her most of the way. After she excused herself to get dressed, Carrie overheard her papa telling one of the hands to hitch up the buggy for her.

She hesitated for a moment when she saw the bay filly tied to the hitching rail. She was high-strung and Carrie didn't quite trust her. Still, Gretchen would be with her, and if she said anything to Papa, he might change his mind about letting her go.

The wind whipped Carrie's long skirt around her legs as she untied the horse. The little filly rolled her eyes and pranced to one side.

Carrie was used to the wind that blew almost continuously on the Kansas prairie, and paid it little mind as she climbed into the buggy, took a firm grip on the reins, and settled into the seat. "You'd better calm down before Papa, or Mac, or Cyrus see you," she said softly.

The bay did seem to grow calmer in response to her voice. By the time they reached the end of the lane, she was plodding along as sedately as an old plow horse. As soon as they turned onto the main road—and were out of sight of the ranch house—Carrie loosened her hold on the reins. The filly tossed her head and broke into a smooth trot. Carrie relaxed and began composing a mental list of the errands she needed to attend to in town.

If Lucille wasn't in such a hurry to get married, they wouldn't be so rushed to get everything done. As it was, Carrie and Gretchen had only a month to get their dresses made, in addition to taking care of the myriad details that were their duties as bridesmaids.

At twenty, Lucille was two years older than Carrie and Gretchen. Carrie smiled as she thought of her friend, then laughed aloud as she remembered the last night Gretchen and Lucille had spent with her. They always stayed at Carrie's house because Gretchen had so many little brothers and sisters there was no privacy, and Lucille's mother was so finicky they couldn't have any fun at her house.

It had only been a few months ago.

Wearing long white flannel nightdresses and heavy winter robes, the three friends went out to the kitchen, popped corn and made hot chocolate. At least Gretchen and Lucille did; Carrie didn't know the first thing about cooking. Back in Carrie's room, they sat cross-legged on the bed drinking chocolate and eating popcorn. Talking about clothes and men, they giggled until they were breathless.

Then Lucille, who was overly dramatic, rolled her huge green eyes and flung herself back on Carrie's bed. Crossing her arms over her bony chest, she intoned, "This is how I shall live and this is how I shall die. An old maid schoolteacher, unsullied by the hand of man."

They giggled and pummeled each other with pillows until Mac banged on Carrie's door and told them to quiet down or he was going to make them sleep in the barn.

Now, after a whirlwind courtship, Lucille was going to marry Jedidiah Smith, the new owner of the livery stable. And Gretchen would be next if Billy Racine, Cyrus's top hand, ever worked up nerve enough to ask her.

"I'll be the only one left." Carrie sighed.

It wasn't that men didn't like her. They did. Jake Philips had been in love with her ever since he sat behind her in first grade. She liked Jake, too. He was comfortable. Like an old pair of shoes. She knew everything about him. She even remembered how he used to wet his pants because Miss Finch wouldn't let him go to the outhouse. She wrinkled her pert little nose. She'd rather be a spinster and die "unsullied by the hand of man," as Lucille put it, as to marry a man she knew as well as she knew Jake.

Not that she didn't like men. It was just that she had yet to meet the man of her dreams.

From the year she turned fourteen, Carrie had often day-dreamed about the man who would one day win her heart. His hair was brown—golden brown with a stubborn lock that tumbled over his forehead. He had gentle blue eyes, and his square chin had a slight cleft.

Gretchen and Lucille knew all about him. When they were younger the three girls called him "The Mysterious Stranger," and they spent hours dreaming up adventures in which he was constantly rescuing Carrie from some terrible danger. He was always fearless, courageous, daring, and heroic. In spite of the fact that he could shoot straighter and ride faster than any other man, he was gentle and compassionate. He was also extremely romantic, and the stories always had a happy-ever-after ending.

Carrie sighed. The other two girls had long ago forgotten "The Mysterious Stranger," that paragon of masculine perfection. But Carrie hadn't. She thought of him when she was alone, or had nothing else to occupy her mind. Jake Philips—in fact, all the men she knew—paled in comparison to her dream lover.

The Braun ranch buildings loomed ahead and Carrie urged the little filly into a faster trot. She hoped Gretchen was ready. The wind seemed stronger and she didn't want to get caught in a storm. Papa would never again let her go out alone if she did.

Gretchen was watching for her and came running out the door as Carrie brought the buggy to a halt in front of the house.

She climbed up and plopped on the seat, making the buggy bounce. Her bosom heaved as she caught her breath. Gretchen was blond and tall—even taller than Carrie, who was six inches over five feet—and voluptuous. Her mother had a new baby every two years, regular as clockwork, and Gretchen was always in a hurry and breathless from chasing after so many younger brothers and sisters. Though she said she loved babies, she often told Carrie she never wanted as many as her mother had. In her opinion, three or four were plenty.

Carrie's mother died when she was young, and even though she never suffered from a lack of love, she had been a lonely, only child. She thought the noisy, rambunctious Braun clan was wonderful. Besides, she adored Gretchen's mother. Having been raised by her father and his two partners, she sometimes wondered what she would do without Hilda Braun's wise and sensitive counsel, especially when it came to some of the more intimate aspects of growing up.

Carrie flicked the reins, and the bay took off like she had just heard the starting gun. Gretchen clutched the side of the seat with one hand and clamped the other hand down on her bonnet. "What's wrong with her?" she gasped.

"She's skittish and only about half-broke, I think," Carrie said as she struggled to bring the buggy under control. Finally the little bay slowed to something between a trot and a gallop, and Carrie relaxed enough to say, "I don't know, but I think Papa must have had that new hand Cyrus hired hitch the buggy for me."

"You mean the one that kept wanting to court you? The one you told you didn't keep company with the hired help?"

Carrie nodded, and Gretchen said, "Perhaps you should have been more tactful."

Tactfulness wasn't one of Carrie's strong points. A faint blush touched her smooth cheeks. "I tried," she said, "but Jess didn't seem to understand the word no."

ॐ

The girls spent an hour at the dressmaker's choosing fabric and a pattern from the latest issue of Vogue and being measured for their dresses.

When they came out, the wind had picked up and ominous black clouds were rolling in from the southwest. They hurried through their other errands, then climbed in the buggy and headed out of town.

"Mrs. Wright has been after me to wear a corset ever since I was fourteen. I've always managed to talk her out of it before, but this time she pulled the tape so tight around my waist she almost cut me in two." Carrie wrinkled her nose. "I just know she's going to make my dress so small I'll have to wear one of those awful contraptions to get into it."

Gretchen laughed. "Carrie, you're the only girl I know who has never worn a corset. They really aren't that bad," she soothed. "I've worn a corset since I was thirteen."

Carrie gave her a dubious look. "I don't know." The color rose in her face. "Besides. I don't have one. And I don't know how I'm going to ask Papa." Her face brightened. "Maybe I could borrow one from you."

Gretchen shook her head. "My goodness, Carrie, you can't wear one of my corsets. Not that I wouldn't be happy to loan you one, but you surely noticed when Mrs. Wright measured us that my waist was twenty-four inches. And I'm wearing a corset. Yours was only twenty-two inches without one."

Carrie sighed. "I guess I'll just have to ask Papa."

By the time they reached the Braun's place, thunder rumbled overhead and the black clouds were hanging so low they could almost reach up and touch them.

"You'd better come inside and wait out the storm." Gretchen said.

Carrie shook her head. "If I don't get on home they'll

worry about me. Besides," she inclined her head toward the filly, "she's finally figured out who's boss."

Gretchen collected her purchases and stepped out of the buggy. "I don't know," she said with hesitation lacing her voice. Carrie followed her gaze to see the little bay rolling her eyes and prancing nervously.

"I'll be all right," Carrie said. She touched the reins lightly to the filly's back and she bolted forward.

The sky darkened to a threatening black, and lightning flashed in the west as she pulled onto the main road. Carrie thought about turning back to wait out the storm, as Gretchen had suggested. But, when the bay tossed her mane and picked up speed, Carrie realized it would be impossible to turn her; she had her hands full just trying to keep her on the road.

The wind jerked her bonnet off and long strands of auburn hair blew across her face and eyes. Just then, an especially powerful bolt of lightning streaked down, striking a large tree along the side of the road directly ahead of them. The little bay danced backward, crying out in fear, then bolted off the road.

Carrie was thrown back against the seat as the buggy cleared the ditch, but she quickly righted herself. Realizing she had lost all control, she hastily wrapped the reins around the stock, and concentrated on staying in the buggy until the filly ran herself out.

A jagged streak of lightning struck the ground nearby and a deafening clap of thunder ricocheted across the prairie. A wild scream tore from the bay. Beside herself with fear, she reared on her hind legs pawing the air, then jumped to the side, dragging the frightened girl and rocking buggy straight toward a deep gully. Carrie squeezed her eyes shut and hung on for dear life. When she opened her eyes, she saw a tall man on a big black horse riding out of the storm.

He raced past the out-of-control buggy. Then, his gloved hand reached out and grabbed the bridle, turning the bay away from the edge of the gully, and bringing her to a trembling stop.

He looked back at Carrie. "Are you all right, Miss?"

"I am now." She watched as he dismounted. He was tall and broad shouldered. A pearl-handled Colt 45 Peacemaker in a black holster was tied low on his right hip.

As he began to stroke the bay's nose and whisper soothingly to her, Carrie climbed from the buggy. He looked at her and his blue eyes lit up. "I'd say you're more than all right." He grinned.

two

Carrie had seen appreciation in men's eyes before when they looked at her and paid them no mind. But this man was different. She blushed and tried to brush her auburn hair into some semblance of order.

"Thank you for rescuing me," she said.

"The pleasure was all mine." When he smiled and removed his hat, a lock of golden-brown hair fell across his forehead. "You must have been frightened out of your wits." He reached out and took her hand. "Look how you're tremblin'."

She had been frightened, and she was trembling, but not from fear. He hadn't shaved for a couple of days and through the light growth of whiskers she saw a dimple in his square chin.

"What took you so long?" She felt the color rising in her face. "I mean where did you come from? I don't remember seeing you before. Are you from around here?"

"Nope." His grin revealed strong, white teeth. "I'd reckon you could say I'm just a stranger passin' through."

The sky had lightened some, and Carrie realized the sound and fury of the storm had passed. She quickly pulled her hand from his. "I'm sure someone will be out searching for me, Mr. . . . Mr. . . . I don't believe I caught your name."

His blue eyes crinkled at the corners when he smiled at

her. "Thornton," he said. "John Thornton."

"My name is Carrie. Actually, it's Caroline. I was named after my mother."

"Caroline. A beautiful name for a beautiful young lady." His soft drawling accent caressed her name, and sent shivers chasing up and down Carrie's spine. "I think you had best get back inside the buggy, Miss Caroline. I just felt a few drops of rain and I wouldn't want you to get wet."

Carrie hadn't even noticed the big drops splattering around them. She couldn't let him get away. Not now. Not when she'd only just found him. "Our place isn't too far from here," she said. "If you'll follow me home, I know Papa would like to thank you."

"Why, Miss Caroline, I have no intention of lettin' you drive home alone. If you don't mind, I'll just tie Jet to the back of the buggy, and we'll see you safely home."

"No, I don't mind." She couldn't contain a jubilant smile. "As a matter of fact, I'd appreciate it. I'm still a little shaky."

"Just as soon as I help you into the buggy we'll be on our way."

Before Carrie realized his intent, he put his hands around her waist and lifted her into the buggy. Then he tied the big black gelding to the back and climbed in beside her. By the time he had the buggy turned around, the rain was coming down in a torrent. The downpour lasted less than two minutes. The clouds had moved to the east, and the sun was shining brightly when they bounced through the ditch and turned onto the main road.

When Carrie saw three mounted men approaching at a gallop, her heart sank. "That's Papa, and Cyrus, and Billy," she said. "I suppose they're coming to look for me."

John guided the buggy to the side of the road and stopped.

He studied the men as they approached. They were all three wearing loose-fitting slickers, but he could see that the man in the lead was tall and broad shouldered. The second man was considerably older, shorter, and of a more stocky build. The man bringing up the rear looked to be around John's age. He was extremely tall and lanky, and sat his saddle with loose-jointed ease.

The first man reined in and dismounted before the big Appaloosa came to a complete stop. He leaned against the buggy and John saw that, beneath his deep tan, he was pale. "Carrie, are you all right?"

Carrie leaned forward to look around John. "Of course I am, Papa. The storm frightened my horse, and she—"

"I still can't believe that any one could be so irresponsible as to—"

"Oh no, Papa! I thought I could handle her. Really I did."

"I'm sure you did." Her father raised his wide brimmed Stetson and combed his fingers through his thick auburn hair, before clamping the hat back on his head. "We'll discuss your part in this later. Right now I'm talking about Cartwright giving you that filly to drive. If he hadn't got a dose of conscience and gone to Billy when that storm blew in, it's hard telling what might have happened."

Billy, who had remained mounted, winked at her. Carrie thought of pointing out to her father that John Thornton had rescued her, not Jess Cartwright's conscience. But she knew her father and wisely kept her mouth shut.

The older man dismounted and walked around to the

other side of the buggy.

He patted Carrie's arm. "You sure you're all right, Young'un?"

"I'm a little shook up, Cyrus. Otherwise, thanks to Mr. Thornton, I'm fine."

"Well, you don't have to worry about young Cartwright no more. Soon as he told me what he done, I sent him packin'."

"You fired Jess?" Carrie felt a pang of guilt. If she hadn't been so rude to him, none of this would have happened. "I don't think he meant to hurt me."

"That's what he said." Cyrus snorted. "Said he was jist playin' a little joke on you. Well, I let him know in no uncertain terms that we didn't think it was funny."

Cyrus patted Carrie's arm once more before stomping around the buggy and pulling himself into the saddle.

"The main thing is that you're all right." Carrie's father pushed away from the buggy. "But, I think you might as well know now, we're going to make some changes."

"Please, Papa, don't. . . ."

He frowned. "We'll talk about this later, Carrie." He started to walk away, then stopped and looked at John. "My daughter said your name was Thornton, didn't she? Mr. Thornton, would you mind driving Carrie home?"

The younger man had smiled at him, but this was the first time either of the older men had acknowledged John's presence. "No, I wouldn't mind at all," he said, picking up the reins.

"Good!" the other man said, curtly. "I want to talk to you when we get back to the house."

John nodded and guided the little bay back out onto the road. The three men on horseback fell in behind the buggy.

"Oh, boy!" Carrie muttered under her breath. "Now I'm going to get it."

John glanced at her. "Your pa won't whip you, will he?"

Carrie looked at him with wide brown eyes. "Whip me? Papa? Of course not. Mama used to whack me once in awhile, but since she died. . ." She shook her head. "If anybody laid a hand on me, Papa would have their head mounted on a stick."

John grinned. "That's good 'cause I'd hate to go up against your pa. He looks like he can handle himself."

"Well, you don't have to worry about that. He isn't going to whip me, but he's going to do something just as bad."

"What can be as bad as a whippin', Miss Caroline?" He grinned at her. "If I remember right, my pa could make an old peach switch beat a pretty snappy tune on my backside."

"Your pa whipped you?" Carrie gasped. "How terrible!"

John threw back his head and laughed. "He only whipped me when I really needed it, and that wasn't too often. I loved Pa, and I rarely disobeyed him."

"I love Papa, too." Carrie said.

"Who's the old man? Your grandfather?"

Carrie shook her head. "Goodness no. I guess I never had a grandfather. Cyrus and Mac are Papa's partners. Oh, dear!" Carrie sighed. "Mac is really going to have himself worked into a lather."

"Why didn't he come with the others?"

"He can't ride. His horse rolled on him about ten years ago and crushed his leg. Since then he's been our biscuit shooter.

Maybe you can stay for supper. Mac is a wonderful cook."

"Much as I'd like to, Miss Caroline, I have a job waitin' for me and I'm afraid I'll have to be movin' on."

They chatted about inconsequential things the rest of the way to the ranch.

A wispy little man wearing Levi's and a plaid flannel shirt hobbled out of the house as soon as the buggy rolled to a stop. "Where you been, little lady? I walked close to ten mile this afternoon, jist worryin' 'bout you, and with this gimpy leg thet's a fur piece." He glared at John. "Well, air you jist goin' to set there gawkin' or air you goin' to help the little lady down?"

John jumped down and ran around the buggy. He reached up and lifted Carrie from the buggy as effortlessly as though she weighed next to nothing.

Her father and Cyrus walked around the buggy to join them. "Mr. Thornton, in all the excitement we forgot to introduce ourselves. The young fellow back there is William Racine. These are my partners, Cyrus Groves and Mac McDougal." Billy grinned and gave a little salute. The other three men shook John's hand.

"I'm Sherman Butler."

John's hand dropped back to his side and the smile died on his face.

"I have a job offer for you, if you're interested," Butler said.

Of course, they would need someone to replace Jess! Carrie's face lit up.

Surely John would forget the job he was going to and stay. Mac grasped her arm. "I baked somethin' special fer you, little lady. Jist come on inside while they's talkin' business."

Carrie tried to catch John's eye as Mac hurried her away, but he refused to look at her.

＆

That night, John left the bunkhouse and walked out to the corral. After he checked on Jet, he stood in the shadows and looked toward the sprawling ranch house. A couple of hours ago, sixteen men had gathered for supper around the long table in the kitchen. Billy told him that Sherman Butler and his foreman rarely ate with the men—preferring to dine with Butler's daughter—but tonight both he and Cyrus had been present, one at either end of the table.

Funny how things worked out. If a wrangler hadn't been snubbed by Miss Butler and chosen to get revenge. . . If it hadn't stormed. . . If he hadn't just happened to ride along when he did. . .

He had expected it to take days to track down Butler. Instead, Sherman Butler had been dumped right into his lap. Not that he was so crazy about the job he'd accepted. Playing nursemaid to Butler's daughter wasn't going to be easy.

He hadn't seen Caroline after the little man dragged her off to the kitchen. Billy said she didn't fraternize with the hired help. Well, that suited him just fine. She was too beautiful for her own good. Certainly too beautiful for his good. If he wasn't careful, Miss Butler could lead him down roads he would not allow himself to travel.

One by one, the lights in the house were extinguished. John turned and headed back to the bunkhouse.

three

When Carrie woke the next morning, she stretched luxuriously, then curled down under the covers. Last evening, watching from her window while John turned his big black gelding into the corral with the other horses, she knew he was staying.

She also knew Papa didn't want her to mingle with the hired hands. He said it would only cause trouble. She had spent the evening trying to think of a way to make Papa see that John was special, and they should spend time together, without letting him know how much she liked him.

It was funny how it had all worked out without her having to do anything.

Last night when Papa had come to tuck her in, he had sat down on the side of her bed and had taken her hand in his. "Caroline Abigail, you could have been killed today. You have always come and gone as you pleased, but from now on, you are not to go out alone. Do you understand?"

She understood all right. Papa had called her by her full name. That meant she wasn't going to like what he had to say. She knew he was going to take away her freedom. And all over some vengeful, love-struck cowboy. It wasn't fair! "But, Papa, it wasn't my fault. Jess Cartwright—"

Papa cut her protests short with a shake of his head. "While Jess Cartwright is mostly at fault for what happened today, you must accept your share of the responsibility. You made some very poor decisions, little girl. When you saw that filly at the hitching rail, you should have asked the boys to hitch up another horse for you. Having failed to do that, you should have taken shelter at the Brauns's until the storm was over."

"But, Papa, I thought I could handle her. Really, I did."

A slight smile tugged at the corner of his mouth. "I'm quite sure you did. But, you must realize that you can't always handle things. Sometimes an older, wiser head is required. That's why I've hired John Thornton. He is to escort you everywhere you go."

After all her scheming and plotting it was to be this simple?

Her father patted her hand. "I'm sorry, Carrie, I know how much you value your freedom, but this is the way it's going to have to be from now on."

Carrie scooted down in bed and turned her face into the pillow. "Does he have to go with me every morning when I ride Brandy?"

"I'm afraid so, Honey." Her father stroked her arm as he spoke. "I don't want you to go anywhere without him. Tomorrow morning, I'm sending him out with Billy. After that, Mr. Thornton will be at your beck and call."

He had kissed her, told her again how sorry he was, then left the room.

Just thinking about John Thornton this morning brought a smile. In fact, she'd probably smiled all night while she slept. She jumped from bed and ran to the window. John and Billy were just riding out. Well, Billy could have him today, but after that, he was all hers. Carrie twirled away from the window. As soon as she got dressed, she thought she'd go for a ride.

❧

John and Billy rode all morning, checking cattle, and looking for breaks in the fence. About noon, they stopped at a line shack. "We might as well sit at a table to eat." Billy grinned.

John shrugged his shoulders. "I'd reckon it beats eatin' on the ground."

They left the horses to graze, and John followed Billy into the cabin. Two bunks were built against one wall. A rickety table and two straight chairs occupied a second. A wood-burning stove with a pile of firewood took up the third wall beside it.

"All the comforts of home," Billy said, brushing a spider off the table, along with a thick layer of dust.

"I've seen worse." John set the sack of hardtack and beef jerky Mac had given them that morning on the table. Then he pulled up one of the chairs.

He started to reach for the sack, but stopped short when Billy bowed his head. Last night at supper he'd been surprised when the men joined hands around the table while Butler prayed. Then, this morning, Butler hadn't been there, but one of the other men prayed. Now, Billy was praying. John shook his head. He couldn't figure what Butler was trying to pull. Trying to pass himself off as a God-fearing Christian, he supposed. Well, he might be able to fool some people, but he couldn't fool John Thornton.

Billy looked up and grinned. "There's a few don't hold

much with prayin' and Bible readin'. Cyrus, he's the foreman, don't require it, but him and Mr. Butler and Mac is all believers and so is most of the men."

"My folks set quite a store on the Bible and prayer, too," John said.

"That so?" Billy's dark eyes reflected his interest. "Your folks is Christians then?"

"Yeah." John took a big bite of hard tack and washed it down with a swig of water from his canteen.

Billy chewed for a minute. "My pa wasn't much on religion, but my ma took us young'uns to church ever Sunday."

John kept eating.

"I didn't listen to her much after I got a little older," Billy continued. "Guess I kinda figured all that church stuff was for women and little kids. Then, one night I went out with a bunch of fellas. We started drinkin' and shootin' up the town. We didn't mean no harm—we was just havin' ourselves some fun—but the sheriff and his deputies took the destruction of public property serious. Anyway, they shot one of the fellas and the rest of us ended up in jail."

"That's too bad," John said, interested in spite of himself.

"Yeah! Well, I didn't kill my friend, but I felt responsible for his death. Sittin' there in that jail cell I finally realized if I kept to the path I was on I'd end up on a coolin' table just like him. When I got out of jail, I decided it was time to make a fresh start. I come here to the Circle C lookin' for work. When they told me they didn't allow no drinkin', nor swearin', nor gamblin', that was fine with me. Drinkin' was what got me in trouble in the first place. I never wanted to see a bottle of whiskey again as long as I lived."

He took a swig from his canteen then wiped his mouth on the back of his hand. "Anyway that was six years ago. It took me awhile to start goin' to church, but finally I begin ridin' in with Mr. Butler and the other men. One Sunday mornin' I made a decision that changed my life. I sure wasn't plannin' to walk down that center aisle, but seems like the Spirit just reached out and shook me, and this voice inside me said, 'Now's the time, Billy Racine,' and the next thing I knew—"

"This is all very interestin'." John pushed his chair back from the table. "But I think it's time we were movin' on."

Billy grabbed up the empty sack and followed him outside.

The two men mounted up and rode west. The sun was warm on their heads and a gentle breeze stirred the tall grass. John turned and looked at Billy. "Butler's got hisself a good size piece of ground here."

Billy nodded. "Four hundred square miles, or thereabouts, I reckon."

Two hundred fifty-six thousand acres. John stared straight ahead, his eyes hard, his face set. "Men like Butler are driven by greed. The more they've got, the more they want, and they don't care how they git it."

"Some, maybe," Billy said. "But, not Sherman Butler and his partners. They started out with nothin', just like me and you. They worked hard for ever'thing they got."

"That so?" John raised a disbelieving eyebrow.

"Sure is," Billy said. "They hitched up together after the war and drifted to Texas. You're a Texan yourself, ain't you?"

John nodded but offered no additional information, and Billy continued with his story. "Anyway, they stayed in Texas awhile, gathered up a herd of longhorns, and drove them up the Chisholm Trail in '71. Land here was pretty easy to come by then, and this is where the market was, so they just stayed. Mr. Butler had left his wife and baby in Texas. After a year he had a cabin built and was settled in, so he went back for them. His little boy died when he was three. His wife, Miss Caroline, never was real stout, and she died before I come here. Miss Caroline was a real lady, I reckon, and Mr. Butler loved her somethin' fierce. The Circle C's named after her, you know. They've expanded over the years, but I don't reckon it's come easy."

John had listened without comment to Billy's narrative. Now he said, "Well, I reckon we don't all see Butler the same way."

"Sherman Butler is one of the finest men I ever knew." Billy defended his boss.

"I'd reckon there's people in Texas would disagree with you," John said, spurring his horse forward.

They spent the rest of the afternoon mending fence and checking cattle.

They made a good team. Billy liked to talk, and John didn't mind listening.

Late in the afternoon, Billy shaded his eyes and squinted toward the sun. "Must be 'bout four o'clock. Guess we'd better be headin' back. Mac don't take kindly to folks bein' late for supper."

John nodded, and the two men mounted up.

They hadn't been riding long when they topped a rise,

and John saw a small grove of trees. He pointed. "Looks like an old homestead."

Billy nodded. "Yep, it is. Wanna take a look?"

John shrugged. "Sure. Why not?" He nudged Jet forward, and Billy followed.

When he drew closer, he saw that the trees were an orchard. He dismounted by the ruined foundation of what had been a small house. A huge tree a short distance from the house provided pleasant shade in the summer.

Billy followed him when he walked over and looked up into the spreading branches of the tree. "Looks like a kid might've had a swing here," he said, pointing up at some frayed scraps of rope swaying in the breeze. John nodded, then turned, and walked away. He paused beside a bed of iris that had been planted against the burned out foundation of the house. "I wonder how long ago the house burned."

Billy lifted his hat and scratched his head. "Ten-fifteen years ago, I reckon." He replaced his hat. "It was before I come here. I reckon the folks didn't live here more than a year or so before the house burnt. They must've planted the orchard. The apples just begin bearin' a couple a years ago."

John nodded, then began to walk to the orchard with Billy tagging at his heels.

"The people that lived here is buried right over yonder," Billy said. "Come on! I'll show you."

This time Billy led the way. John stood beside the fence that surrounded the well-tended grave and looked down at the tombstone. "Who put the stone here?"

Billy scratched his head. "I don't rightly know. Mr. Butler, I reckon."

John read the inscription aloud. "In memory of the Nolan family. John. Mavis. And their son, Lucas. Died—August 21, 1880."

John turned, and he and Billy walked back to their horses. The two young men mounted up, nudged their horses into a gallop, and without a backward glance headed toward the bunkhouse and supper.

four

After watching John and Billy ride out, Carrie quickly made her bed and straightened the room, then dressed in a soft, tan, full-sleeved shirt, and a brown, ankle-length, divided skirt. She plaited her long, auburn hair into a single braid, and pulled on riding boots. Snatching up a cream-colored, roll-brimmed Stetson, she went to the kitchen.

Mac's sleeves were rolled up past his elbows, his hands and forearms submerged in a large pan of soapy dishwater when she came through the door swinging her hat by the chin strap. Andy Clark, the gangly teenage boy who helped him in the kitchen, was taking the clean dishes from the rinse water, drying them, and then putting them away. They both turned and looked at her. Andy's slightly blemished young face was suffused by an expression of unabashed adoration.

Mac frowned. "Where you think yer goin' in thet git-up, little lady?"

"I'm taking Brandy out for a short run." Carrie grabbed for a biscuit and Mac slapped at her hand with a soapy spatula.

"You set yourself down there to the table and eat yore breakfast proper, young lady," he growled.

"Haven't got time." Carrie put her hand with the biscuit behind her back, out of Mac's reach.

"You got all the time in the world." Mac dried his hands on the dishtowel and reached for a clean plate. "Set down and I'll rustle you up some grub."

"All I want is some of your delicious apple butter for my biscuit." Carrie looked at him appealingly. "Please, Mac."

"What kind of breakfast is thet fer a growin' girl?" Mac grumbled as he handed her a clean spoon.

"I haven't grown an inch in the last two years," Carrie reminded him, as she moved to the table and spread a generous layer of apple butter on the biscuit.

"Thet's why yer so skinny," Mac said. "If you'd eat proper you'd put some meat on them scrawny little bones."

"I'm not scrawny, am I, Andy?" Carrie smiled at the boy, and his face turned bright red all the way up to the roots of his sandy hair.

"No, Ma'am! I think you're the purtiest girl in the whole world."

"Purty is as purty does," Mac growled. "And you ain't goin' nowheres, little lady. Didn't yore pa tell you from now on you ain't leavin' the place 'thout John Thornton goes with you?"

"He told me. But Mr. Thornton rode out with Billy awhile ago."

"Then I reckon you'll jist have to wait 'til he rides back, won't you?"

"Papa said Mr. Thornton would start riding with me tomorrow morning. If I go out this morning, I'll have to go alone."

Carrie knew her father had left the ranch earlier so felt perfectly safe adding, in an aggrieved tone, "If you don't believe me you can ask him."

"I ain't questionin' yore word, little lady, but we talked 'bout this yesterday, and we's in agreement you wasn't to go anywheres alone. Yore pa never told me nothin' 'bout yore goin' out alone this mornin'. But I'd reckon if you don't go fur. . ."

Carrie knew the battle was won and she threw an affectionate arm around the little man's shoulders. "Thanks for the biscuit, Mac. I won't be gone long." She leaned down slightly and planted a kiss on his bristly cheek.

"You don't have to go gettin' all mushy on me." He rubbed the spot she'd kissed. "I reckon it'll be all right this time, if you don't go fur."

"I'd be right proud to go with you, Miss Carrie," Andy said.

"I know you would, and I really appreciate you offering." Carrie's arm dropped from Mac's shoulders. "Maybe some other time." She reached up to pat the boy's cheek as she walked past. "You're turning into a right handsome young man, Andy."

❧

Andy stood next to Mr. McDougal and together they watched as Carrie went out the door munching on her biscuit.

" 'She walks in beauty like the night,' " Andy murmured.

"What's thet you said?"

The boy's face colored. "Nothin', Mr. McDougal. Just somethin' I read in a book."

"She walks in beauty as the night," Mac said softly. "Yep, I reckon she does. And so did her ma." He turned his face away for a moment before turning back to scowl at Andy.

"I ain't payin' you to gawk at the little lady and spout nonsense from sum book. Now get back to work!"

ᴓᴬ

An hour after she left the ranch, Carrie slid from Brandy's back beside a small pool of crystal-clear water. This was her oasis. Her secret place. She had stumbled across it a couple of years ago and had immediately claimed the spot for her own. A sparkling stream, running swiftly through a grove of trees, cascaded over the rocks in a shimmering waterfall. The dancing water hesitated only long enough to feed the deep pool before spilling over the side and passing swiftly on its way. Carrie found something almost magical in the calm pool with the madly rushing water on either side. The pool was a constant in her life, a circle of serenity.

She knelt on the thick, velvety moss and leaned over. The pebbles on the bottom seemed to lie just below the surface of the water, but Carrie knew the pool was much deeper than it appeared. Once she had tried to measure the depth with a long, slender stick, but had been unable to touch the bottom.

The reflection of the drooping willows formed a frame for her face. Carrie had never been overly concerned with her looks, but now she carefully studied each feature. She liked her eyes. They were big and dark with long, sweeping lashes. The same eyes that looked back at her from the framed portrait of her mother that hung over the fireplace. Her mouth was shaped like Mama's, too. Only it was wider and her lips were fuller. She decided she didn't like her mouth. It was too big. Her nose was short, straight, and pert. She didn't like her nose at all. She had inherited the deep dimples in her softly rounded cheeks and her auburn hair from her father. She liked the dimples and had always thought her hair was nice, but today she wondered if it was too red.

She sat back on her heels and sighed. There was nothing she could do about her face. You just had to take what God gave you and make the best of it. Andy had said she was pretty. She wondered if John thought she was pretty. He'd seemed to think so yesterday, but maybe he'd only been nice because she was—as Lucille always portrayed her in the stories they used to make up—a damsel in distress.

Brandy nudged her shoulder and she scrambled to her feet. "I know," she said, as she took up the reins, "it's time to go home."

❧

The next morning John and Carrie rode together. Some distance from the house they topped a rise. Carrie stopped to let John, who had been trailing several feet behind, catch up. She swept her arm in a wide arc. "Don't you love the view?"

He looked out over the valley below but remained silent.

"The ranch house and all the outbuildings look like a child's toys from up here, don't you think? Look," she pointed to the right of the Butler ranch, "that's the Braun's place over there. Gretchen is one of my best friends. Lucille Jacobs is my other best friend, but she's marrying Jedidiah Smith next month. Gretchen and I are going to be bridesmaids. I was coming from the dressmaker when you saved my life."

Unnerved but undaunted by his silence, Carrie babbled

on. "I've known Gretchen and Lucille practically forever. Lucille has an older sister. Her mother is so prissy about everything, but Gretchen's mother is wonderful. She has ten children! Isn't that a lot? Gretchen's the oldest. You know Billy?" She giggled. "Well, of course you do. You spent the whole day with him yesterday. Well, anyway, Billy and Gretchen are sweethearts." Carrie paused to catch her breath.

John turned his head and looked at her with eyes as clear and blue as the sky overhead. "Oh, really? Billy talks almost as much as you do, and he never mentioned a sweetheart to me."

"He didn't?" Carrie frowned. "I certainly won't tell Gretchen. It would break her heart if she knew he wasn't talking about her. She would think he didn't love her."

His gaze returned to the scene spread out before them. "Men have private thoughts, Miss Butler."

Carrie's dark eyes flashed. "Are you implying that women don't have private thoughts?"

"I don't know, do they?"

Carrie's face flamed. She kicked Brandy in the sides. The mare was a full sister to the runaway bay, and didn't need any encouragement to run. Before John realized what was happening, Carrie was racing down the opposite side of the hill.

He watched for a moment as Brandy streaked across the prairie with Carrie leaning low over her neck. "Well, Jet, I reckon we'd better go get them before that fool girl breaks her neck."

Carrie heard the thunder of hoofbeats behind her and

urged Brandy on. Glancing over her shoulder, she saw them bearing down on her. She knew Brandy, good as she was, was no match for the big black. Sitting up, she reluctantly reined in.

Jet shot past her then slowed. John turned him with a motion of his body and brought him back to stand beside Brandy. "There's no way that little bay could ever beat Jet, no matter how long her pedigree is."

Carrie's pert little nose shot up in the air. "We could have beat you. We just didn't want to."

His laugh was mocking. "I've never seen anything—thoroughbred or otherwise—that could beat Jet. Certainly not that little fancy-dancy mare."

Carrie drew herself up to protest, and John interrupted. "We'd better get back to the barn so I can rub these horses down."

"I take care of Brandy myself, thank you." Carrie pulled the little mare around and headed for home.

John trailed behind, watching her erect back. She sat well in the saddle, poised and alert to her mount. Carrie Butler was more woman than he had first suspected.

◆

They rubbed the horses down in silence. When they led them out of the barn, John said, "If you've had your fun for today, I'm goin' to work."

"Fine." Carrie smiled up at him. "Since tomorrow is Sunday, we won't ride, but you will be expected to have the buggy hitched at eight-thirty sharp and escort me to church."

"I don't go to church, Miss Butler, so I'm afraid I must refuse your polite request."

She realized she had sounded a trifle bossy and flushed. "I'm sorry I was rude, but Papa said I was not to go anywhere without you. How am I supposed to go to church if you refuse to escort me?"

"I've heard that almost everybody here goes to town for church on Sunday morning, Miss Butler." He tipped his hat. "I would suggest you ride with your father." He gave her a jaunty little salute and walked away.

Carrie glared at his retreating back. Things certainly weren't going as she had planned. Yesterday when she met him, he seemed interested in her. Today he didn't act as if he even liked her. Her face lit up as a slow smile spread from her full lips to her eyes. John Thornton was the man she was going to marry, whether he realized it or not. And sooner or later he would take her to church.

five

As soon as Butler and the entourage from the Circle C left for church the next morning, John saddled Jet and rode out to the west. He watched carefully for familiar landmarks until, topping a gentle rise, he looked down on the old homestead he'd visited on Friday.

He reined Jet in, hooked his leg around the saddle horn, and studied the peaceful scene below him for a short time before kicking his foot into the stirrup and urging Jet down the slope. He dismounted beside the ruins of the foundation and let the reins drop to the ground. The big black lowered his head and began to graze on the tender new grass.

Taking his knife from the scabbard at his waist, John knelt and dug up three of the iris growing beside the old foundation stones. He carried them carefully through the orchard. The fence that enclosed the grave had been put there to keep cows out; it was not so high that he couldn't step over. He knelt and planted the iris. When he was finished he stood looking at the tombstone for several minutes, then stepped back over the fence.

The black gelding was where he had left him. He mounted and rode up the slope the way he had come.

❧

Carrie could hardly wait to tell Gretchen and Lucille about John Thornton. But by the time Mac had parked the buggy, the church bell was pealing out, calling the faithful to worship.

Lucille was on the other side of the church, seated between her parents and Jedidiah. She glanced up when the Butlers slid into their pew, and Carrie waved. Lucille raised her hand in a discreet salute. Mrs. Jacobs frowned at Carrie and poked a sharp elbow into her daughter's ribs. Lucille quickly dropped her hand and turned her attention back to the pulpit.

Carrie, settling down between her father and Mac, wrinkled her nose. Mrs. Jacobs was such a grouch. Poor Lucille! No wonder she'd been in such a hurry to get married. Living with that woman would be practically impossible.

Only one pew separated her from the Brauns. Billy was sitting with Gretchen almost directly in front of her. If only it weren't for the pew between them, she could whisper to Gretchen when they stood for the opening hymn. Since that was an impossibility, she'd have to write a note and figure out someway to pass it to her.

When her father, who was seated next to the aisle, went forward to pass one of the collection plates, Carrie began to rummage through her small handbag for a pencil. Mac nudged her gently and when she glanced up, he scowled at her. She tried to look as innocent as possible, but Mac shook his head slightly before taking her purse and putting it on the seat between him and Cyrus.

Carrie sighed in defeat, then picked up her Bible. She'd just have to wait until after church to tell Gretchen and Lucille about John. Wouldn't they be surprised!

From the number of amens and praises uttered that

morning, Brother Carson must have preached a rousing sermon. Carrie wouldn't have known. Although she tried to look attentive, her mind was elsewhere.

After church, Lucille's mother whisked her away before Carrie had a chance to talk to her. And by the time she made her way through the congregation to Gretchen, the Brauns were ready to go. She managed to pull her friend away from Billy only long enough to say, "I've met him, Gretchen! The most wonderful man in the world. The man I'm going to marry."

"Oh, Carrie, how exciting. I wish I had time to hear all about it, but Billy's coming to our house for dinner." One of Gretchen's little brothers grabbed her hand and tugged toward where Billy and the rest of her family were waiting. "I'm going to have to go before Karl pulls my arm off. Come over as soon as you can and tell me all about it." And with those few words, Gretchen was gone.

Things hadn't worked out at all as she had planned, and Carrie was feeling decidedly grumpy when her father lifted her into the buggy beside Mac. The Circle C crew, including her father and Cyrus, was merely a cloud of dust in the distance by the time Mac pulled out of the churchyard.

"I wish I could ride Brandy to church instead of being stuck in this poky old buggy." Carrie knew she sounded like a whiny five-year-old, but she didn't care.

"Yer jist a might peevish today, ain't you?" Mac looked at her from beneath beetled brows.

Carrie scowled back at him. "Nothing went right this morning."

"Thet ain't true, little lady." Mac shifted the reins to his left hand and made a sweeping gesture with his right arm. "Jist you look at all the beauty the Lord has surrounded us with. And, if'n thet ain't enough, He's allowed us to spend these last few hours in His house. They's lots of people would give their eyeteeth to have what we enjoyed today. Ain't thet right?"

Carrie shifted restlessly on the buggy seat. "Yes, Mac. I am thankful for all that I have, but still. . ."

Mac took the reins in both hands, and they rode in silence for the next mile. Finally, Mac said, "Thet was a mighty fine sermon Brother Carson preached this mornin'." He glanced at Carrie. "Didn't you think so?"

Carrie squirmed in her seat. "Yes, it was. Very inspiring," she murmured.

"If it were so inspirin'," Mac said as his faded blue eyes seemed to look into her heart, "what was it about?"

"You mean the topic?" Carrie looked everywhere but at the old man. "Well, I think it was about Jesus and. . .and. . . Nicodemus," she finished triumphantly. "It was about being born again."

Mac grunted. "You was either payin' more attention than I thought, or you jist made a lucky guess."

"I was listening," Carrie muttered.

"No you wasn't. You did more squirmin' round than a flea on a hot stove. Church is fer worshipin', little lady, not fer woolgatherin'. You'd best be rememberin' thet."

Sunday was a bad day for Carrie. Mac scolded her. She didn't catch a glimpse of John all day. And worse even than these things, she hadn't been able to talk to her friends. She knew she would burst if she didn't tell Gretchen about the wonderful turn her life had taken only four days ago.

Monday morning started off on a promising note. John was almost civil when Carrie told him of her plans to go to the Brauns'. Though he didn't say anything to her on the ride, she was encouraged.

When she turned in at the Brauns' gate, John followed. She stopped at the hitching rail and dismounted.

John stayed in the saddle. She tipped her head back and looked up at him. "Aren't you going to get off your horse?"

"I'll be back for you in a couple of hours." John turned Jet and started back down the lane.

How were Gretchen and her mother going to see him if he just dumped her on the doorstep like some unwanted parcel and rode away? "I thought you'd wait for me."

He glanced back over his shoulder. "I reckon you thought wrong, Miss Butler. I'll be back in two hours."

Carrie wrapped the reins loosely around the hitching rail while she watched him ride away. "Sometimes I'd like to shoot him," she muttered in Brandy's ear.

Gretchen's mother—an older, plumper version of Gretchen—opened the door, a small baby cradled in one arm. She reached out and drew Carrie inside with her free arm. "Gretchen told me last night that you had met someone special." She peered over Carrie's shoulder. "Where is your young man going? I thought you'd bring him in to meet us."

"He had some things to do. Perhaps when he comes back for me. . ."

The baby had been fussing, now he began to howl.

"You'll have to excuse me, Carrie. This one wants his breakfast. Gretchen's in the kitchen feeding the little ones."

Carrie found her friend shoveling oatmeal into a balky two year old, at the same time she was urging two tow-headed little boys to eat. "I can talk as soon as I get these three fed," she said, as she hurried by on her way to the stove. "Katy is overseeing the bed-making. Soon as she's finished she'll take over here, and we can visit." She plopped a steaming cup of tea on the table. "Here, sit down and drink this while you wait. And try not to spill it."

Carrie sat sipping her tea while her friend dashed around, alternately shoveling food into her little sister's mouth, wiping up the two boys' messes, and washing dishes.

Carrie didn't know how Gretchen did it, but by the time her tea was finished, she had fed all three children, washed and dried the dishes and put them away, and had the kitchen in order.

Fourteen-year-old Katy came to relieve her, and Gretchen and Carrie escaped to the bedroom Gretchen shared with Katy and the two year old. The room was already in order, so Gretchen dropped into a chair. Not seeming to know what to do with her idle hands, she picked up a crochet hook and a ball of thread and began to work on a half-completed doily.

"So, tell me all about him!" she said.

Carrie quickly told Gretchen how she met John. Then, she concluded by saying, "He rode out of the storm and rescued me, and I knew as soon as I saw him that he was the man I would marry."

Gretchen had been listening very carefully and without

comment. Now she lay her crocheting to one side. "I don't know, Carrie. You say he's very handsome. Are you sure you aren't just drawn to him because he's good-looking?"

"Of course not." Carrie drew herself up indignantly. "I'm not a flighty female who falls in love with the first man who looks her way."

"I didn't say you were," Gretchen said. "It's only that this man is a stranger to you. You didn't even know he existed four days ago."

Carrie laughed. "But that's the wonderful thing. The first time I saw John I felt this flash of recognition. It was like I had known him forever."

"But you haven't, Carrie." Gretchen leaned forward and fixed her luminous blue eyes on her friend. "Where did he come from?"

"Texas." Carrie replied, promptly. "See! I do know something about him."

"But, not enough. Does he have any family? For all you know he could have a wife. And, if he is from Texas, what brought him here?"

"I think God brought him here so we could meet. And if that's true, then he couldn't have a wife. Now, could he?"

"That brings up the most important question of all. What are his beliefs? Is he a Christian?"

"I don't know. I only know that I love him. I thought you'd be happy that I had finally found someone."

"Oh, Carrie, I love you. And I want to be happy for you. But, please! Please! Ask some questions."

Carrie nodded. "If you think it's that important, I will."

The two girls spent the remainder of their two-hour visit

talking about the wedding. Katy tapped on the door to announce, "There's a man on a big, black horse outside, Carrie. Is he for you?"

"Yes, he's for me," Carrie answered and grabbed her hat. "Now, you'll see him," she told Gretchen, "and when you do, you'll understand why I love him."

But by the time the girls came out on the porch, John was already halfway to the main road. He appeared to be waiting for her, but not too patiently.

At the end of the lane he fell in behind her and remained there until Carrie reined Brandy in and turned in her saddle to look at him. "Why don't you ride up here so we can talk?"

He stopped a horse length behind her. "We have nothin' to talk about, Miss Butler. Besides, I was told that you didn't fraternize with the hired help."

"I don't usually, but if we're going to spend time together, it would be nice if I knew something about you."

"We aren't keeping company, Miss Butler. I'm being paid to do a job, and I'm doing it. If my work isn't satisfactory, perhaps you should find someone more to your liking."

Every one of his carefully enunciated words struck at her heart with the force of a physical blow, but she managed to smile. "I find you quite satisfactory, Mr. Thornton." Then, remembering Gretchen's admonition to find out more about him, she said, "But there is one thing I would really like to know."

He cocked an eyebrow, which she interpreted as permission. "Are you married?"

"No, Miss Butler, I am not, nor have I ever been married. A man in my line of work can't afford the worry of a family."

She wanted to ask what his line of work was, but before she had the opportunity, he said, "Miss Butler, I suggest we head back to the ranch. I have work to do, even if you don't."

She nudged Brandy and they galloped the rest of the way home a full fifty feet ahead of the man on the big black gelding.

❧

John left Carrie at the barn rubbing down the little bay and rode to the west. He spent the remainder of the day mending fence and checking what cattle he came up on. There was always a threat of fire on the dry prairie, but the danger was intensified in the spring when the high winds could fan the smallest spark into a raging inferno and send it sweeping across hundreds of acres in a matter of hours, destroying everything in its path. He had seen several prairie fires and kept a constant watch for smoke.

Of necessity, John had lived a solitary life. He had never minded the loneliness before, but today the image of a beautiful redhead with a mouth made for kissing was never far from his thoughts.

That evening after supper, John sat in the bunkhouse listening to the other men talk. They had tried to draw him into conversation the first couple of days. He had been polite enough, but at the same time, he held himself aloof, rarely speaking unless addressed directly.

Only Billy still went out of his way to be friendly. The

others had taken in his appearance. The short-barreled Colt Peacemaker 45 with the well-worn grip tied low on his narrow hip. The Winchester .44-.40 with the calibrated rear sight he carried in the scabbard on the big black gelding. The steely watchfulness of his blue eyes. His taciturnity.

They considered all these things and put him down as a man with a past he was trying to forget. A gunfighter. Or, a man on the run. Most of them had been in the same position at one time or another and, without animosity, allowed him his privacy.

When one of the men picked up his guitar and began to strum a familiar tune, John felt the room closing in on him. Feeling as though he were suffocating, he walked out the door.

He paused to breathe in the cool, early spring air. Then, as a man began to sing, he walked to the corral. The words followed him. "Amazing grace how sweet the sound. . ."

Jet came to the fence and nudged his shoulder. He stroked his horse's neck and Jet whoofed contentedly. Even over the soft sound of the horse, he heard the familiar words.

Pushing away from the corral, he walked to the barn where he could no longer hear the guitar or the sound of the man's voice. But the words of the old hymn were not so easily escaped. From the deepest depths of his memory a sweet feminine alto sang: "The Lord has promised good to me; His word my hope secures; He will my shield and portion be as long as life endures."

He regained his composure as he stood in the shadows watching the ranch house. One by one, the lights were extinguished. He thought of the girl in one of those darkened rooms. And, he thought of her father, and of the job that had brought him here. Finally, he returned to the now silent bunkhouse.

six

Determined to put John Thornton out of her life, Carrie gave up her morning rides. For the remainder of that week, she stayed close to the house, only leaving to ride into town with her father on Sunday. During her self-imposed exile, she caught glimpses of John and silently berated herself when her heart leapt. She was a fool! John Thornton would never love her. He didn't even like her. By week's end, she knew that, while she might put the good-looking wrangler out of her life, it was not going to be so easy to put him out of her heart.

Sunday night after her father tucked her in and put out her light, she decided her room felt a bit stuffy and got up to open the window. Breathing in the clean air, she lifted her eyes to the heavens. It was a beautiful night. Millions of pinpoint diamonds of light lit the dark velvet sky.

The spring after her mother died, her father had been too wrapped up in his own grief to comfort her, so Cyrus and Mac had stepped in to fill the void in her life. She remembered sitting on the porch on Cyrus's lap. They had talked about Mama and about heaven where Mama lived now. While they talked, he had pointed out the different constellations to her.

Now, ten years later, she remembered and searched the heavens for the constellations. The Big and Little Dipper were easy. Some of the others were more difficult, but finally, using the Big Dipper as a reference, she found them. Leo, the lion. Gemini, the twins. Arcturus. And, lastly, Virgo, the virgin.

As she turned away from the window, a small movement in the shadows beside the barn caught her eye. Someone was standing there watching her window. Instinctively, she knew that the figure was John. She waited for several minutes before returning to her bed.

❧

Early the next morning, her resolve to win John's love rekindled, she burst into the kitchen where her father sat eating his breakfast. "Papa, Mrs. Wright told me at church yesterday that our dresses are ready for the first fitting. I need John to escort me into town this morning." She bent and kissed his cheek. "Will you have him hitch the buggy for me?"

He set his coffee cup down. "Sit down and eat, Carrie."

"But, Papa, we need to go early and. . ." She dropped into her chair. "Those pancakes do look delicious. I guess I have time for one, Mac."

Mac turned from the stove and frowned at her. "You been moonin' round here all week like a dyin' calf in a hail storm. No more than you been eatin' one pancake ain't even a start, little lady." He limped over and set a steaming stack in front of her. "You clean these up!"

She grinned up at him. "If I eat all these I'll be too fat for my dress for sure."

The old man cuffed her affectionately, then limped back to the stove.

A huge pat of yellow butter was already melting and running down the sides of the golden brown stack of pancakes. Carrie added warmed sorghum.

Between luscious mouthfuls, she talked. "Just wait until you see me in my dress, Papa."

His pride was evident in his smile. "I'm sure you'll outshine the bride."

"Papa!" She scolded. "That wasn't nice. Lucille is really quite attractive."

"I was not passing judgment on the bride's beauty, little girl. I was simply remembering your mother and thinking how much you look like her. Caroline was the most beautiful woman in Texas. I never could understand why such a fine lady agreed to hitch up with a penniless wrangler like me."

"I know why, Papa." Carrie's voice was subdued. "And I'm glad you think I look like her. But I'm also glad I have your red hair and dimples."

Cyrus chose that moment to come in the back door. He patted Carrie on the head. "Did you leave anything fer me, Young'un?"

"There's plenty left, but I ain't goin' to wait on you." Mac grunted, and sat down at the table.

Cyrus took a heaping plate from the warming oven and joined them. "Well, I reckon they won't kill me," he said.

"Them are the finest pan cookies you'll ever put a fork to," Mac grumbled. "If you'd stuff your mouth 'stead of runnin' it, you'd know that."

The two old friends exchanged several insults before they bowed their heads and offered thanks. Carrie, remembering she hadn't prayed, dutifully bowed her head.

When she raised her head, her father was looking at her. She smiled sheepishly. "I guess I was so excited about going to town I forgot."

"Seems to me you've been fergettin' a lot lately," Mac muttered.

The three men exchanged glances. Then her father said, "You will be stopping by for Gretchen, won't you?"

"Oh, yes! She'll need to try her dress on, too. That's why I forgot—about praying, I mean—I was excited about spending the morning with Gretchen."

She looked down at her plate. "There's one more thing, Papa." A faint pink tinged her cheeks. "I have to have a. . ." She raised her head and looked from her father to Mac to Cyrus, to Andy—who had been sitting across the table gazing at her with worshipful eyes ever since she sat down— then back to her father. "Mrs. Wright says I have to have a. . .a corset."

Andy's face was even redder than hers as he got up and hastily left the room.

"Is that so?" Her father shook his head. "What's Mrs. Wright trying to do? Make a grown-up lady of my little girl?"

Carrie glanced at Cyrus and Mac, expecting some comment, but they were suddenly busy with their pancakes.

"It's the dress, Papa. I tried to convince her to make it looser, but she insisted that wouldn't be stylish. I won't be able to button it at the waist without one."

Her father's expression grew thoughtful. Carrie had only been eight when her mother died, but she had come to recognize that faraway look in her father's blue eyes. He was thinking about Mama. "When Caroline knew the end was near, she had me pack some things to keep for you until you were older."

The thought of her mother thinking of her while she lay dying brought tears to Carrie's eyes. She impatiently brushed them away.

"I'll go tell John to hitch the buggy. While you're gone we'll put the trunk in your room. If what you want isn't there, I'm sure Mrs. Wright can supply the necessary item of apparel."

Carrie pushed her chair back. "You finish your breakfast. I'll find Mr. Thornton."

John wasn't difficult to find. He was leaning against the barn picking his teeth with a straw.

She greeted him with a wide smile. "You are to hitch up the buggy and escort me to town."

He straightened and threw the straw aside. "Certainly, Miss." He tipped his hat. "I live to serve your every whim."

Her smile faded. "Hitch up the little bay. The one I was using the day of the storm."

"Really?" His smile was insolent. "Sure you can handle her?"

She had intended to ask him to drive her, but his arrogance brought out her stubborn streak. An angry flush tinted her smooth cheeks. "You aren't being paid to question my orders," she snapped, and immediately wished she could recall her hasty words.

A muscle jerked in his cheek as he choked back an angry retort. Turning on his heel, he stalked to the corral. Taking a coiled rope from the fence post, he effortlessly lassoed a placid brown mare.

She started to make a caustic remark about his lack of ability with a lasso, but bit back the words and stalked into the ranch house while he hitched the mare up to the buggy and saddled Jet. On the drive to the Brauns', he rode just far enough behind the buggy to make conversation difficult, if not impossible.

When they reached the Brauns', John dismounted and handed Gretchen into the buggy. He even smiled at her. A nice friendly smile, not the superior smirk he reserved for Carrie. Then, he resumed his silent vigil several hundred feet behind the buggy.

As soon as he was out of earshot Gretchen clutched Carrie's arm. "Oh, Carrie! I can't believe it." Her blue eyes danced with excitement. "He is 'The Mysterious Stranger.' Right down to the dimple in his chin. Only he's even more handsome than we imagined."

Carrie glanced at her friend. "I didn't want to say anything before for fear it would be prejudicial, but you can see it, too." She turned her attention back to the road. "The only problem is, I don't think he likes me much."

"Oh, Carrie!" Gretchen squeezed the other girl's clenched fist. "Of course he likes you. How could he not? After all he is 'The Mysterious Stranger.' "

"I don't know." Carrie shrugged. "Everything I say or do makes him angry."

"Oh, I see." The other girl smiled knowingly. "You had a little tiff."

It wasn't little, and it was much more than a tiff. But Carrie straightened her back and lifted her chin. "Gretchen, if it's the last thing I do, I'm going to marry John Thornton."

"Oh, I don't know about that, Carrie." A slight frown creased the other girl's smooth forehead. "I mean the 'Mysterious Stranger' was just made up, like in a fairy tale. John Thornton is a real, live person."

"I know," Carrie giggled. "Isn't it wonderful?"

"But like I said before, Carrie," Gretchen said, glancing over her shoulder at the man trailing their buggy, "you don't know anything about this man."

Carrie laughed. "Of course I do. After we left your house on Monday, I asked him about himself, just like you told me to."

"Oh, good." Gretchen visibly relaxed. "Then he is a Christian."

Carrie shifted in the seat. "Well, that's not exactly what I asked him."

"Why not?"

"Well, my goodness, Gretchen, that's a pretty personal question." She slanted a glance at her friend. "Don't you think?"

"I most assuredly do not think so." She shifted in the seat to face Carrie. "Exactly what did you ask Mr. Thornton?"

"I asked him if he was married. And he's not." She favored the other girl with a triumphant smile. "So there."

"If John Thornton doesn't share your faith, you'd best just forget him. After all, he's not the only man in the world."

"No," Carrie's brown eyes were serious. "But he's the only man I will ever want."

"Carrie, you know what it says in the Bible about being unequally yoked together with unbelievers."

"You worry too much, Gretchen." Carrie reached out and patted the other girl's arm. "We've never had an argument in our life. Let's not quarrel about this."

She flicked the reins and the horse broke into an easy canter.

≈

John watched until the two girls were in the dress shop before leaving to attend to some personal errands.

Carrie tried her dress on first. No matter how much she sucked in her breath, it failed to meet around the waist.

Mrs. Wright clucked disapprovingly. "You simply must have a corset if your dress is to fit properly, Carrie."

"I know and I will have one," Carrie promised. "I'm going to look for one in Mama's trunk this afternoon."

"Caroline was a beautiful lady. She wouldn't have dreamed of venturing out without a corset." The dressmaker's plump face relaxed in a relieved smile.

"I'm sure she had several."

"We will turn up the hem and pin it today. When you come for your final fitting be sure and bring the corset." She adjusted a few gathers. "I think this will do quite nicely once you have the proper foundation garment."

Carrie twirled in front of the long mirror, being careful to not step on the unhemmed skirt. "I think it's lovely, don't you, Gretchen?"

"Yes, it's very pretty," Gretchen agreed.

"Try yours on while Mrs. Wright turns up my hem!"

When Gretchen stepped out from behind the screen, Carrie caught her breath.

"You are so beautiful, Gretchen."

The other girl blushed. "You've just never seen me in anything this fancy."

The dressmaker stepped forward and made a few minor adjustments. "You see what a difference a corset makes in the fit?" she said.

Even with a corset, Gretchen's waist was a couple of inches larger than hers, but Carrie nodded her head. The corset did make a difference. "You've done a wonderful job, Mrs. Wright."

The dressmaker beamed her appreciation.

seven

John was just riding up when the girls emerged from the dressmaker's shop.

"Where have you been?" Carrie asked as soon as he dismounted. Though it was obvious from his freshly shaven face where he'd been.

"I've been to the barber shop, Miss Butler." His blue eyes were cold. "I didn't realize I needed your permission to go for a shave and a haircut."

"No. . .no, you don't," she stammered. "I just meant you look so. . .so. . ." Breathtakingly handsome was the phrase that came to her mind. "Much nicer," she finished lamely.

John scowled at her, then turned to the other girl with a smile that rivaled the noonday sun.

"Miss Gretchen?" He handed her into the buggy, then putting one foot in the stirrup, swung lightly into the saddle, leaving Carrie standing in the street.

He tipped his hat. "As soon as you are ready, Miss Butler, we'll be on our way."

She climbed into the buggy and picked up the reins with trembling hands. The buggy moved out into the street and John fell in behind.

It began to sprinkle just as they rode into the Butler's barn lot, and it showered intermittently the rest of the afternoon. That night the heavens opened, and rain fell for several days.

Confined to the house, Carrie's dark mood matched the stormy weather. Her father had brought her mother's trunk in and left it in the corner of her room. She found the corset on top, underneath a large Bible, but she didn't have the energy to explore further. She removed the corset, replaced the Bible, and closed the lid.

She spent the rest of the week sleeping and moping around the house. She whiled away one whole afternoon sitting on the couch gazing at the portrait of her mother that hung above the fireplace. In the portrait, her black hair was loose and cascaded down over her shoulders in shimmering waves. Her smooth dark skin, large soulful eyes, and high-bridged nose spoke of the touch of Spanish blood that flowed through her veins. A hint of a smile played at the corners of her well-shaped mouth.

Carrie tried to remember her. She had fragments of memory of her mother before she got sick. But most of her memories were of a beautiful, frail woman who spent most of her days in the big bed in Papa's room. She could remember the soft silkiness of a nightdress. A light flowery scent mingled with a medicine smell. The gentleness of a thin hand on her hair. Her mother had slept more and more that last winter. Then one morning she didn't wake up. A week later she died.

She couldn't remember the funeral. Only that she had cried and cried. And Papa hadn't. He had drawn his grief around himself like an impenetrable cloak. Finally, he had gone away for a week. When he came back, except for the sadness that still lingered in the depths of his blue eyes, he was the attentive, loving Papa she had always known.

Where had Papa been that week? She went to the only person she thought might give her an answer.

Mac was sitting in a rocking chair in front of the massive fireplace with his bad leg propped up on a footstool. She pulled up a chair facing him and sat down.

He laid aside the newspaper he'd been reading and peered at her over the round wire-rimmed glasses that perched on the tip of his nose. "You look like you'd been sent fer and couldn't go. What's ailin' you, little lady?"

"I've been looking at the portrait of Mama. When Papa left after Mama's funeral, where did he go?"

Mac took off his glasses, reached into his pocket, and pulled out a large bandanna. First, he scrubbed at his eyes then polished his glasses until they shone. "That fireplace must be smokin' agin."

He pushed himself out of the chair and picked up the poker. Carrie sat patiently while he poked at the fire.

Mac put the poker back in its stand by the fireplace, and hobbled over to the cabinet. "When we first come here we cooked in thet fireplace. We didn't have nothin' like this here stove back then."

Carrie knew the huge black and chrome range was Mac's pride and joy, but she didn't want to hear about it. "Where did Papa go, Mac?"

"I got work to do, little lady. Why don't you just have a slab of this here chocolate cake I baked in the oven of my nice range, and forget them questions?"

"But, I really want to know where. . ."

"Your pa took his Bible and a jug of water and went up to one of the line shacks. Now, get you a piece of this here cake and quit pesterin' me."

"Forevermore, Mac! I'm not a child. I want to know, what did he do up there? Please, Mac," Carrie's big brown eyes begged. "You're the only one who ever tells me anything."

"Humph!" Mac snorted, but there was a pleased expression in his faded blue eyes.

Carrie pressed her advantage. "What did Papa do at the line shack?"

"I'd reckon he found somethin' he'd been a-lookin' fer a long time." Mac tied a large white apron around his skinny middle. "If'n yer goin' to stay here pesterin' you might as well peel spuds."

Carrie pushed her chair back under the table. "I'll just leave," she said, and swept majestically from the room.

&

The rain ended the next afternoon and the warm May sun made its welcome appearance. Carrie found John in the small corral with a bronco. The animal was already snubbed down to the breaking post and John was standing in front of the big red gelding, stroking his neck, and talking softly to him.

Carrie hadn't seen this gentleness in John since the day he rescued her, and she stood quietly watching, until he looked up and saw her. He ambled across the corral to her. "Is there somethin' I can do for you, Miss Butler?"

"Gretchen and I need to go into town. Will you hitch the buggy up, please?"

"I'll have it ready in half an hour. I would like to clean up a bit before we go. If that's all right with you."

Carrie nodded, and went in the house to wait. He hadn't seemed overly happy to see her, but at least he hadn't been rude. Maybe John had missed her this past week, as much as she had missed him.

☙

Gretchen and Carrie spent the night before the wedding with Lucille. They were too excited to sleep, and the three friends laughed and talked until well into the night.

The next morning, Lucille's mother hovered over her daughter, helping her dress. Carrie, knowing that her own mother would never see her in her wedding dress, felt a twinge of sadness, but she quickly put her selfish thoughts aside. This was Lucille's day.

Gretchen laced Carrie's corset so tight she protested. "Gretchen! If you pull those strings any tighter, my eyes are going to pop out! Then I'll never trap John."

The other two girls giggled, but Lucille's mother clicked disapprovingly. "Young ladies do not trap husbands, Carrie."

She turned to the other two. "Lucille, you and Gretchen are dressed. I would like to speak with Carrie in private. Would you mind going into the spare room to finish your primping?" She glanced at the small clock on her daughter's dresser. "We will only be a few minutes."

"Yes, Mama." Lucille gathered up her skirt and left without a backward glance.

Carrie rolled her eyes. This wasn't the first lecture she had received from her friend's mother.

Gretchen smiled at her sympathetically before pulling

the door closed behind them.

"Carrie, it has been my intention to speak to you for some time, but with planning the wedding and all. . ."

"I know we've all been very busy," Carrie murmured in agreement. "But you most of all," she added hastily. "I know most of the work has fallen on your shoulders, and you've done a marvelous job."

Flattery might work with Mac and Cyrus and her father, but Mrs. Jacobs was made of sterner stuff. "Your mother was a beautiful woman, Carrie."

"Yes, she was," Carrie agreed.

"Caroline was not merely beautiful on the outside, she had a beautiful spirit as well. Your mother loved the Lord with all her heart, Carrie. She was a good and faithful servant right up to the day she died."

"That's what Mac told me," Carrie said.

"I feel very fortunate to have been friends with your mother, Carrie." Mrs. Jacobs lifted a delicately embroidered hanky to the corner of her eye. "Did you know Caroline led me to the Lord?"

Carrie shook her head. She hadn't known.

"Well, she did. Then I was able to bring Nels, and later our two girls to a saving knowledge of Jesus Christ. I will be forever grateful for what Caroline did for me and my family."

Carrie thought of the Bible in her mother's trunk. "I think I remember Mama reading her Bible."

"I'm quite certain you do. Caroline read her Bible faithfully. She was the one who impressed on me how very important it was to find time every day to read the Word and pray. A quiet time, she called it. A time to be alone in communion with our Savior." She patted Carrie's arm. "That is one of the things I wanted to talk to you about, Carrie. I know your mother would want you to follow her example. How long has it been since you sat down and really read your Bible?"

"I read my Bible," Carrie protested. "Maybe not every day, but I don't always have time."

"You are an avid reader, Carrie. You find time to read novels. You find time to ride. You always have time to visit your friends. Why do you have time for the wood, hay, and stubble of this life, but no time for the gold and silver? The things of eternal value."

"I go to church every Sunday."

"Yes you do. And, that's a credit to your father and his two friends. Sherman has done a wonderful job of raising you, Carrie."

Carrie dug the toe of her slipper into the rug. "I love Papa, and Mac, and Cyrus."

"I'm quite sure you do." Mrs. Jacobs took Carrie's dress from its hanger. "I'll help with your buttons while we finish our little talk."

She slipped the dress carefully over Carrie's upswept hairdo. While Carrie adjusted the folds of the skirt, the older woman stepped behind her and began to work the tiny buttons through the looped buttonholes.

"They love you too, Carrie. So much so, that they can't see your faults. Therefore, I feel it is my duty to have this talk with you. I doubt that you have ever cooked a meal in your life. Your housekeeping duties consist of making your own bed. And, worst of all, I fear church has merely become a place you go to socialize. I was there when you and Gretchen went to the altar. My heart rejoiced when you two girls were saved. Gretchen has matured into a fine Christian young woman, but you, Carrie. . .I don't believe you have grown in your faith one iota."

Carrie glanced pointedly at the clock.

"Yes, we have to go in a few minutes." Mrs. Jacobs slipped the last button through its loop. "You are of a marriageable age, Carrie. Surely you want a husband and babies. . .every woman does."

She put her hands on Carrie's shoulders and turned the girl to face her. "It takes more than a pretty face and figure to attract a suitable husband. A man wants a wife with a sweet, submissive spirit—a godly woman he can depend on to manage his home and raise his children."

Mrs. Jacobs began to gather up her things, and Carrie sensed freedom. "Thank you for talking to me, Ma'am. If you are finished, I think I'll go see if Lucille needs me." Her hand was on the doorknob when Mrs. Jacobs reached out to put a restraining hand on her arm. "There is one other thing, Carrie—this John Thornton you are so infatuated with."

Carrie groaned inwardly. She should have known she wasn't going to get away so easily.

"I haven't seen young Mr. Thornton in church even once since he's been here."

"John is a good man," Carrie protested weakly.

"Good is not enough," Mrs. Jacobs frowned. "We, as Christians, are not to be unequally yoked together with unbelievers. It is best you forget this man, Carrie." She released the younger woman's arm, allowing Carrie to escape at last.

Finally, dressed in their wedding finery, they rode to the church in the Jacobs's buggy.

While the bride and groom exchanged vows, Carrie's thoughts drifted to John. Would they ever stand where Lucille and Jedidiah were standing now? Would John ever look at her with love in his eyes, and promise to cherish her forever? Lucille's mother said men like to feel protective toward a woman. She said if Carrie ever wanted a young man to love her, she was going to have to behave in a more ladylike manner. Maybe Mrs. Jacobs was right. Maybe she would have to learn to act helpless, and flirt, like some of the girls she had gone to school with, such as Becky Colton. She certainly had no trouble attracting any man who caught her eye.

"You may kiss the bride," the minister's voice interrupted Carrie's musings.

She watched as her friends exchanged a tender kiss, and her determination to become a lady was strengthened. As soon as she got back to the ranch, she was going to introduce John Thornton to the new Carrie Butler.

&

John was on the way to the breaking corral when he saw the Butler's buggy coming up the lane. He stopped in front of the barn to watch as Butler reached up and lifted Carrie down. She scanned the barn lot, then walked slowly toward him. As she came closer, he saw that she was wearing something frilly and green. The dress set off her upswept red hair and flawless, lightly tanned skin to perfection. He couldn't control the rapid beat of his heart, but he managed to keep his face an expressionless mask.

She greeted him with a wide smile. "Oh, Mr. Thornton, you should have been at the wedding."

"I've been to weddin's, Miss Butler. In my experience they are all pretty much the same."

"Oh, but this one was different." Her eyes sparkled. "You'll never guess what happened."

It was almost impossible to not respond to her, but he managed. He'd spent a lifetime hiding his feelings. "No, I don't reckon I will. I was never good at playin' games, Miss Butler."

Carrie refused to let his indifference dampen her spirits. "Billy proposed to Gretchen and she accepted." She hugged herself and her joy bubbled over. "Isn't that the most romantic thing you ever heard of?"

A long denied emotion stirred inside John. He struggled against it. And won.

"Romantic?" He lifted an arrogant eyebrow.

Carrie caught her breath. He was the most exasperating man she had ever known. "Yes, romantic. Gretchen caught Lucille's bouquet, which means that she will be the next one married. And Billy walked up to her right then and there and asked her to marry him. Right in front of all the wedding guests. Practically the whole town was there."

"Practically the whole town, huh? Well, I guess with that many witnesses old Billy is hog-tied, and as good as branded." An amused smile tugged at the corner of his mouth before he could suppress it. "I'll be sure to give the poor fellow my condolences."

Carrie was sure she had seen him smile. Just a hint of a smile. But a smile nevertheless. Remembering her resolve, she batted her eyes and giggled. "Why, Mr. Thornton! What an absolutely horrible thing to say."

John looked at her a bit strangely. "If you don't need me, Miss Butler, I have a wild bronco waiting for me." A sudden, overwhelming urge to show off for her gripped him. "Perhaps you'd like to come watch."

Carrie's heart jumped, then she remembered. A real lady would never hang on a corral fence cheering on a bronco-buster. "My goodness, Mr. Thornton." She fluttered her eyelashes at him. "The breaking corral is no place for a lady."

"Fine. Have it your way, Miss Butler." He tipped his hat and started to turn away."

"Mr. Thornton." He turned back to face her. "Please be careful," she said softly.

The gaze of her dark eyes caught and held his for one precious moment. Then he touched the brim of his hat and walked away.

eight

Carrie watched John climb over the corral fence before turning toward the house. She wished she could have gone with him. But since she couldn't, her top priority at the moment was to change into some more comfortable clothes.

As soon as she was in her room, she began struggling and straining to undo the row of tiny buttons down the back of her dress. She'd had misgivings about wearing a corset, but the spark of interest she had detected in John's blue eyes made it seem worthwhile.

She finally unbuttoned the last button and slipped the dress off her shoulders, letting it fall to the floor. She looked at herself in the mirror and was pleased with what she saw. She realized the corset emphasized her small waist and full bosom, but besides the fact that it was terribly uncomfortable, she couldn't wear anything she couldn't put on by herself. Mrs. Wright had said her mother wouldn't dream of leaving the house without her corset. In this womanless household, how had Mama managed to lace herself up?

"Of course," a faint blush touched her cheeks, "Papa must have laced her corset."

She reached behind her back and struggled to undo the laces that Gretchen had pulled so tightly. She breathed a sigh of relief as she folded the corset, and laid it on top of Mama's trunk to be put away later. When she hung her dress in the wardrobe, she rifled through the other garments hanging there. She hesitated over a navy riding skirt, then selected a more feminine green gored skirt and a matching shirtwaist in a green print.

She had just finished dressing when the activity outside drew her to the window. She pulled the lace curtains aside. A billowing cloud of dust rose in the breaking corral. A group of men sat on the weathered rail fence, or leaned against it, calling encouragement to the man on the wild bronco.

Captivated by the excitement, she sank to the floor in front of the open window. With her arms crossed on the low windowsill, she was able to catch only an occasional glimpse of the man and the horse. The breaking of wild broncos was as much as part of ranch life as roundups and branding. She had sat on the corral fence watching dozens of horses broken with never a thought for the man in the saddle, but this time was different. Even knowing this must be the final breaking of the big red gelding, she expected the rider to be thrown at any moment. A thrill of fear passed through her along with a silent prayer, *Please, Lord, don't let John be hurt.*

John stuck to the saddle like glue—the breaking rope wrapped around one gloved hand, the other hand uplifted—while the horse twisted and turned in a futile attempt to remove the man from his back.

Finally, the bronco came down in a series of stiff-legged, bone-jarring leaps that failed to unseat the rider. Cheers rose from the watching men as the big gelding trotted around the inner periphery of the corral. Someone swung the corral gate open and the horse and rider—the conquered and the conqueror—galloped through and disappeared in a cloud of dust.

The crowd around the corral broke up as the men returned to their duties. Carrie saw her father, Cyrus, and Mac walking toward the house, and quickly moved back, letting the curtain drop. The three men were involved in earnest conversation as they approached her window and Carrie unabashedly eavesdropped.

Her father said, "I'd say that young man has proven his abilities."

Cyrus nodded. "He knows his job all right, and seems to enjoy it."

"Enjoys it too well, if you ask me. I wouldn't trust him fur as I could throw 'im, and with this gimpy leg that ain't fur," Mac grumbled.

"Have you had trouble with him?" Sherman frowned down at Mac.

"Nuttin' you could put yore finger on," Mac admitted grudgingly. "I jist don't like the way he looks at the little lady when he thinks nobody ain't watchin'."

"You been hangin' over that fancy stove too long." Cyrus snorted. "The heat's affectin' your brain."

The men stopped walking almost directly in front of the window where Carrie stood hidden behind the lace curtains.

"Carrie seems so pleased with the arrangement, I guess I never thought he might be thinking of her as more than just a job," Sherman said. "But I'm her father, and sometimes I forget she's not a little girl anymore."

He sounded worried, and a trill of fear shot through

Carrie. What if her father took John away from her?

"You ain't got a thing to worry about," Cyrus scoffed. "I've been watchin' Thornton when he's with Carrie. He's no more interested in her than Billy is."

Carrie wrinkled her nose. Cyrus was half-right. Billy at least liked her. Sometimes John Thornton treated her like she was his worst enemy.

"This old fool's been readin' too many of them dime novels," Cyrus said.

"Wouldn't hurt you to do a little readin'," Mac growled. "Might broaden yore horizons."

Ignoring his friend's final remark, Cyrus said, "Young Thornton's been here a month. He's proven himself a fine hand. I'm thinkin' it's time we told him he had a job."

"Yer the foreman," Mac growled. "I'm jist a biscuit shooter. Reckon yer the one with the final say. But I still says there's somethin' not quite square 'bout that young man."

"Then that's settled." Carrie's father sounded relieved. "You talk to him first chance you get, Cyrus. You might keep an eye on him when he's with Carrie," he added almost as an afterthought.

"I ain't worried 'bout Thornton's behavior with Carrie," Cyrus said, over a mumbled remark of Mac's. "But I will keep an eye on him. There's things about him that jist don't add up. Fer instance, you know I always tried to take care of the Nolan's grave." The men began walking away, and Carrie only caught a fragment of the next sentence. "Well, somebody's been messin' around out there, and I got a hunch. . ."

The three men moved out of earshot, and Carrie whirled

away from the window. Dropping down on her bed, she lay back and spread her arms wide. Mac said John was interested in her as more than just a job. Her heart sang.

She lay there for several minutes thinking of ways she could get John to declare his feelings for her. Although she had grown up in a household composed of men, she knew so little about them. Lucille's mother had chastised the way she acted and said she needed to be more feminine. And she was willing to try, but there had to be more to catching a man than that. She remembered Gretchen's mother saying the way to a man's heart was through his stomach, but Mrs. Braun was a wonderful cook. Carrie couldn't boil water.

She sighed. It might take years before she learned to cook. If only her mother were here. Papa had adored Mama. But she remembered him saying one time that her cooking left something to be desired.

Carrie sat up on the bed. Her mother had been gone so long she sometimes seemed like only a dream, and Carrie seldom thought of her unless she was going through some totally female crisis. Lately, however, she had been thinking of her a lot.

She saw the corset lying on the trunk. Papa said Mama had left special things for her. Maybe there was something in the trunk that would help her.

She rose from the bed and dropped to her knees in front of the leather-bound trunk. Almost reverently, she lifted the lid. A scent of roses and lavender wafted out from the sachet bag tucked in the corner of the trunk, and the light fragrance brought with it an especially vivid memory of her fragile, dark-haired mother.

A large Bible rested on top of the trunk's contents. With deliberate care, Carrie opened the book to the inscription page and read that her father had presented it as a gift to her mother on their first wedding anniversary. Carrie discovered inside the Bible's flyleaf a heavily embossed envelope on which her mother had written, *My Beloved Daughter*. She withdrew the card from the envelope and read, *"To everything there is a season, and a time to every purpose under heaven."*

Carrie replaced the card, then ran her hands lovingly over the rich leather cover before laying the Bible to one side.

She took a small box from the trunk, opened the lid, and lifted out a pale blue, embroidered silk reticule. Three things were inside the dainty handbag. A pressed rose. A dance card filled with men's names—none of them her father's—and another cream-colored envelope with Carrie's name inscribed on it with her mother's delicate script. The card inside proclaimed, *"A time to dance." My first grown-up party. Houston, Texas, April 6, 1865.*

She lifted the next item from the trunk and her eyes widened in wonder. It was her mother's wedding dress. She stood holding the white satin and tulle garment at arm's length, then crushed it to herself, and turned to face the full-length mirror. What would John think when he saw her in Mama's dress on their wedding day? Would he think that she was beautiful?

She turned to lay the dress across the bed and noticed another cream-colored envelope on the floor. It must have been concealed in the folds of the dress. Carrie's name was written on the front. She opened it and read, *"A time to love"—June 9, 1869.* The day her parents were married. She returned the card to the envelope, and laid it on top of the dress.

The next item was a tiny white christening dress with a matching bonnet. She began searching for an envelope with her name on it this time and saw it almost immediately. The card inside said, *Sherman Matthew–March 10, 1871.* And, below that her name and birth date. *Caroline Abigail–March 16, 1874.* Then, *"A time to be born."*

The final envelope—this time edged in black—contained a dark, silky, lock of hair tied with narrow, black ribbon. The card read, *A curl from Matt's first haircut.* And, beneath that, *"A time to mourn"—December 9, 1873.*

Carrie knew about the brother who had died of pneumonia three months before she was born. Had even seen a photograph of the chubby, dark-haired baby. But, until she held the lock of hair in her hand, he had never seemed real to her.

Now, a pain stabbed through her heart at her own sense of loss, and the realization of her mother's anguish at losing her firstborn. She wiped her eyes before beginning to replace the items in the trunk.

Finally, she closed the lid, but remained on her knees beside the repacked trunk. Surely, Mama had left her these things for a reason. Was it to bring her comfort? What had Mama meant by the cryptic messages she had left behind? If only she were here to explain.

Overwhelmed by an almost unbearable yearning, Carrie rested her head against her mother's trunk and wept.

nine

One bright June morning, instead of following their usual route, Carrie turned to the west. After a few miles, John rode up beside her. "You headin' somewhere in particular?" he asked.

She gave him a sunny smile. "As a matter of fact I am. Just over that far rise, there's an apple orchard. About this time of year I like to check on the apples."

He scowled. "Why?"

"I like to see how big they are. When they're ripe I pick them. Mac makes apple butter and the most delicious pies you ever tasted."

"I can save you a trip. It's too early for apples to be ripe."

"I know that, but I like to go there, anyway. There's something peaceful about the orchard." She slowed Brandy and turned in the saddle so she could look at him. "Is there some reason you don't want me to go?"

He shrugged. "It's no concern of mine where you go."

"Good!" A roguish grin flashed across her face, as she forgot her resolve to be more ladylike. "Bet I can beat you there." She kicked Brandy in the ribs and shot ahead of him.

John watched her long auburn braid swing against her slender back as she bent low over Brandy's neck. She had a good head start before he whispered, "Go get her, Jet!" and gave the big gelding his head. Effortlessly, Jet closed the distance between them.

For the blink of an eye, they rode side-by-side. Then John nudged Jet forward and left Carrie behind. He didn't slow until they topped the rise and he looked down on the old homestead.

He was leaning nonchalantly against the trunk of the large high-branched tree when Carrie rode up and slid from Brandy.

"You won!" She laughed, and her dimples flashed. "We had a bet. What is my penalty to be?"

John grinned mischievously. "I'll think of something suitable." Then he remembered who she was, and his smile disappeared. "If you're going to look at the apples, you'd best be doing it. I haven't got all day."

His sudden shift in mood hit Carrie with the force of a blow. Trying to regain the playfulness she'd seen in his eyes before that blue curtain of indifference lowered, she said, "I bet you didn't know that's the hanging tree you're leaning against."

"The hangin' tree?" A spark of interest softened the coldness of his eyes. He stepped away from the tree and looked up at the wide-spreading limbs above his head. "Billy never said anything about it."

"Well, he probably doesn't know." Carrie's eyes were on his face. "It happened a long time before he came here."

"What happened?"

"I'm not really sure," she said, her voice reflecting her eagerness to hold his attention. "But I know some men were hanged here."

"What did they do?"

"I don't know." Carrie's voice faltered, as the old familiar mask of indifference began to descend over John's features. "I don't believe I ever heard."

"Probably owned a piece of land some rich man wanted," John said.

A chill ran down Carrie's backbone at the expression on his face. "I'd better go look at the apples," she said. She turned quickly and walked away.

John watched her go, and the pain in his heart was almost more than he could endure. It had been years since he had allowed himself to love, but he knew that he loved Carrie Butler. He also knew that she could never be a part of his life. As soon as he finished the job he had come here to do, she would want no part of him—would in fact, hate him—and he would move on.

Until then, he had to stay away from Carrie.

He lifted his head and saw her walking among the apple trees. Every now and then, she lifted her hand to pluck a tiny apple from a tree. There was something so completely feminine, so familiar about her gestures that a lump formed in his chest and rose into his throat. How many times had he seen his mother walk through their orchard back home in Tennessee, exactly as Carrie was doing now? Thinning, she had called it. Removing the small, malformed fruit from the tree so that the perfect little apples would have room to grow.

A longing for his mother welled up within him. He passed Carrie without so much as a glance and went to the grave. He stood by the fence and looked down at the roughly carved words on the tombstone.

"This grave has been here for as long as I can remember."

Carrie's soft voice startled John, but he didn't give any out-ward indication that he was aware of her presence.

"Cyrus takes care of it," she said. "I didn't know he had planted flowers though." She stepped around John and knelt at his side. Reaching through the fence, she sifted the dirt through her fingers. "They really need a drink," she said, "especially the rose bush. See how dry the soil is?"

John, still not trusting himself to speak, nodded.

"Will you bring some water?" She stood and looked up at him with pleading eyes. "I hate to see anything die. I think there's an old well here somewhere. If we can find it, we can water them."

John turned without a word and walked to the well that was hidden by the tall grass. He pushed the heavy plank cover aside and dropped the rusty bucket into the wide well. It landed with a splash.

While he pulled the bucket up, he admired the workman-ship of the well. The man that was buried in the orchard, and his son, had spent many hours digging the well, then collecting the rocks that lined it. In silent testimony to the skill and integrity of his craftsmanship, the rocks stood as straight and solid as the day they had been laid.

Something his father had said about the workman being worthy of his hire came to John's mind. Must have been from the Bible. Pa had been a great one for reading the Bible and often quoted passages of scripture. Well, there was only one passage in the Bible that concerned John.

"Whoso sheddeth man's blood, by man shall his blood be shed." Those words had become his creed. He was still a young man, but he had spent a good portion of his life seeking vengeance for people like the Nolans. Fighting fights that were not his. Dispensing justice where justice had been denied.

"Need help?" He hadn't heard her come up, but Carrie stood at his side, a hopeful smile lifting the corners of her soft, full lips.

"I can manage alone." John said brusquely as he swung the bucket from the well onto the rock casing that extended several inches above the ground, forming a low wall.

She followed meekly as he carried the full bucket to the grave, and stood beside him as he let the clear water pour slowly out.

"They're already perking up," she said as the last few drops soaked into the parched earth. "Papa says that's what the love of God does to our souls. It flows over us, soaking into the dry hurting places, and giving new life."

"I'm sure your Papa would know all about that," John said, lifting the bucket over the fence.

He started to turn away as she said, "I don't remember anything about what happened to the people that lived here, but Mama was friends with the woman."

He turned back and looked down at her. Encouraged by the spark of interest she detected in his ice-blue eyes, she babbled on. "I was little when the Nolans died, and I've never heard Papa speak of them, but I remember coming here with Mama a few times. She said they were a good Christian family."

"I thought you didn't remember anything about them," he said.

"Well, I don't. Not really. I mostly remember Lucas, the

son." Her cheeks flushed. "I know you're going to think this is silly, but I was really sweet on Lucas. He was mostly outside with his father, but one time he came in for a snack. I remember there was only one cookie left in the cookie jar, and he gave it to me. Then he patted me on the head and smiled at me, and I was absolutely smitten." A gentle sigh lifted Carrie's shoulders.

"I don't even remember what he looked like, except for his eyes. He had the most beautiful, gentle blue eyes. I remember telling Mama on the way home that when I grew up I was going to marry Lucas Nolan." She smiled a bit sheepishly. "I told you it was silly." She shrugged her shoulders. "I remember I cried and cried when Lucas died."

John looked down at her. "Do you remember anything about the night of the fire?" he asked hoarsely.

"Strangely enough, I do remember that night—although my memories are hazy—because Papa left without kissing me good night. Mama put me to bed and told me to go to sleep. I tried to stay awake, but I finally gave in to sleep. It was almost morning when I heard Papa come in. I remember the sky was starting to get light. I heard Mama and Papa talking in the kitchen. I climbed out of bed because I wanted my good-night kiss. When I got to the kitchen Mama was crying, and I heard. . ."

She paused, trying to remember, and John prompted. "And, what? What did you hear your father say?"

She shook her head. "I don't know exactly what Papa said. I guess he told Mama about the fire. It's what Mama said that I remember. She was crying. I rarely saw her cry and her tears frightened me. I stopped in the shadows just outside the kitchen door. Papa had his arms around Mama. Trying to comfort her, I guess. She was saying, 'I told you it would come to this, Sherman. I told you it had been over for fifteen years. I begged you to let the hate go, but you wouldn't. Now, all those people are dead. That boy! Oh, Sherman, the Nolan boy was only twelve years old.' "

Carrie's hands went to her face and her eyes widened. "Oh, no!"

"What is it? Did you remember something else?"

She nodded. "It was horrible. The most horrible sound I have ever heard. And it frightened me even more than Mama's tears."

"What was? What frightened you? What happened?" He fought the urge to reach out and shake the information from her.

Finally, the words came out. "Papa cried."

ten

The expression on John's face changed so suddenly it was as though a shutter had been slammed closed. His eyes, which only a heartbeat ago had been alight with interest, went cold.

Turning on his heel he stalked away. Numbly, Carrie followed him.

On the ride back to the ranch house, a million questions raced around in Carrie's head.

What had she said? What had she done? She loved this man, of that she had no doubt, but she didn't understand him. And she doubted that she ever would. Why did he have to be such an enigma?

She looked at his broad-shouldered back, for this time he was in the lead, and she had to push Brandy to keep up. She recalled the avid expression on his face when she told him about the hanging tree. Except for the orchard, there was only that one tree at the old Nolan homestead. How had it become known as the hanging tree? Had there actually been men hanged there? Or was it only a story started by a group of cowboys huddled around a lonely campfire? Something based loosely on fact, and exaggerated with each telling until it lost all resemblance of the truth?

She had never been the slightest bit curious, but now she wanted to know. Not just for John, but for herself as well.

That night when her father came to tuck her in, he sat down on the edge of her bed. "And, how was your day, little girl?" he asked, as he had every night for as long as she could remember.

"I rode out to the old Nolan homestead this morning." She pushed herself up against the pillows.

"How are your apples coming along?"

"I think we're going to have a good crop." She plucked at the light blanket that covered her.

His hand closed over hers, stopping its aimless movement. "Is something bothering you, little girl?"

She looked up at him. "Papa, why do they call that big tree the hanging tree? Were some men really hanged there? Or is it just—"

"Forget it, Carrie!" he said harshly, and took his hand away.

"But, Papa. . ."

"That happened a long time ago, little girl." He leaned over and kissed her cheek. "Let it lie."

He put out the light, and left Carrie alone in the dark with a new set of unanswered questions.

Why did Papa avoid the Nolan place? She had asked him to go with her to gather the apples a couple of years ago, but he had said he was too busy. As far as she knew, he had never been to the burned-out homestead. Why? What had happened there? And why didn't he want to talk about it?

She scooted down in bed and turned on her side, facing the window. Through the lace pattern of the curtains, she saw the twinkling stars. She wondered briefly if John was leaning against the barn watching her window, but she didn't get up to look.

The next morning when she went out to saddle Brandy, Cyrus was leading his own horse out of the barn.

"Looks like you got a mighty fine mornin' fer your ride, Young'un," he commented.

"Uh-huh," she answered absently.

Cyrus frowned. "Somethin' botherin' you, Carrie?"

"There is something I'd like to know, if you have a minute."

"I've always got time fer you, Young'un." He patted her arm. "You go right ahead and ask. I'll tell you anythin' you want to know."

Carrie took a deep breath. "I want to know about that old tree out at the Nolan place. The one they call the hanging tree. How did it get its name?"

His face went still and his eyes hooded, closing her out. "It happened a long time ago, Carrie. It don't concern you none. Leave it be, Young'un."

"But—" Cyrus cut Carrie's protest short with a shake of his head.

"I got work to do Young'un." He led his horse out the open door, then turned, and added over his shoulder, "Maybe you best stay away from the Nolan place."

Carrie watched him mount up and ride away. There was one more place to go. She knew she could persuade Mac to tell her what she wanted to know.

❧

"Battin' them big brown eyes ain't gonna get you nowheres with me, little lady." Mac frowned at Carrie. "Whut happened over to the Nolans don't concern you. Now you set yourself down here an' have a glass of milk an' some of these here molasses cookies. They's yore favorite, and I jist took 'em outa the oven of my nice range."

She'd had to wait until afternoon before she was able to catch Mac alone. Now, he refused to tell her anything.

Carrie stomped her foot in frustration. "I'm eighteen years old, Mac. Why do you all still treat me like a child? I can't see why you're all so secretive about what happened. And I don't want your stupid cookies and milk."

She turned on her heel and slammed from the room.

ᴥ

Several times during supper, Carrie caught Papa or Cyrus glancing covertly at her. She picked listlessly at her food. If Mac and Andy hadn't been busy in the kitchen feeding the men, Mac would have been scolding her for not eating.

Finally, she laid her napkin to one side. "I'm not hungry. May I be excused?"

Her father didn't answer but merely nodded his permission. Carrie saw the worried look that he and Cyrus exchanged as she rose from the table and left the room.

An hour later when her father looked in on her, Carrie was already in bed and asleep. He crossed the room and kissed her soft cheek. Then he turned out the light and slipped quietly from the room.

Sometime later Carrie's empty stomach woke her. She hadn't eaten since breakfast. Thinking about Mac's molasses cookies, she slipped on her robe and padded barefoot to the kitchen.

". . .gonna keep askin' questions, 'til somebody tells 'er whut she wants to know."

It was Mac's voice. Realizing he was talking about her, Carrie stepped back into the shadows and listened.

"The only one that would tell her is you," Cyrus said.

"I ain't tellin' her nothin'," Mac said, "but I think mebbe she oughta be told."

"No!" That was her father's voice. She inched closer. "She wouldn't understand. Carrie must never know what happened that night."

"Wal, I think yer wrong, Sherman. Carrie loves us. Ain't nothin' gonna change thet."

"I don't know, Mac. What we done wasn't wrong, but things is different now. The young 'un might not understand."

"I reckon the little lady would fergive us, whether she understood, or not."

"That's not a chance I'm willing to take."

There was a moment of silence, then a chair scraped back. She heard Mac limp across the floor, then a rattling sound, and him limping back to the table. She smelled the coffee as he refilled their cups and her empty stomach twisted.

Finally, Mac said, "I'd reckon young Thornton will be squirin' the little lady to thet party the young folks is havin' for the newlyweds Saturday night."

"I talked to him about it this afternoon. I told him he was to drive the buggy, and leave that big, black gelding at home."

Carrie had so many things on her mind she had forgotten Lucille's party. John was actually going to escort her instead of trailing behind! All thoughts of her empty stomach and of the hanging tree vanished. She crept back to her room and crawled into bed.

It was important that she look her best Saturday night. She mentally inventoried the contents of her closet. Nothing would do, except the green dress she had worn to Lucille's wedding.

She sighed and snuggled down on her pillow. Her dreams that night were sweet.

❧

Carrie knew she was going to need help dressing for the party, so when Billy drove the wagon to town for supplies Saturday morning, she rode as far as the Brauns' with him.

She and Gretchen spent most of that afternoon getting ready. The curling iron never had a chance to cool as they tried several different hairstyles before finally settling on one.

Gretchen's mother found a few free minutes to spend with the girls while they were getting dressed. She sat in a chair watching as they took turns lacing each other's corsets.

"After Lucille's wedding I swore I would never again wear this thing," Carrie gasped, gripping the bedpost as Gretchen pulled the laces tighter.

"You have to get Mr. Thornton's attention somehow," Gretchen said through clenched teeth as she gave the laces an extra hard yank.

"I hope this works, because nothing else has. I even tried to be ladylike for awhile." Carrie felt as though her ribs were about to meet her spine. "Stop, Gretchen! That's enough. I want his attention. But I don't want to die to get it."

"I thought you were going to marry young Mr. Thornton," Gretchen's mother said.

"I am." Carrie was studying her reflection in the mirror. "He just doesn't know it yet."

"I see," Mrs. Braun said, but it was clear from the expression on her face she didn't.

"I knew the first time I saw him that John Thornton was the man I would marry." Carrie wrinkled her pert little nose. "Unfortunately, I don't think he likes me much. But, he will. I'm going to make him love me."

Mrs. Braun shook her head. "You can't make someone love you, Carrie. Love is either there or it isn't. God has given John Thornton a will of his own—just as he has all of us—and this young man's love is a gift only he can give. Even more importantly, Carrie, I don't think Mr. Thornton is a believer. You know the Bible says, 'Be ye not unequally yoked together with unbelievers: for what fellowship hath righteousness with unrighteousness? and what communion hath light with darkness?' I've seen unions like that, Carrie, and they brought nothing but pain and suffering."

The baby began to cry, and Mrs. Braun went to see to his needs.

Carrie knew Gretchen's mother was right. She couldn't force John to love her. Sometimes she wondered why she even wanted to. He was surly, and uncommunicative, and often downright rude. But she had seen occasional flashes of the man underneath.

There had been his open interest the day he rescued her. His gentleness and patience with the broncos he was breaking. The warmth she had seen in his blue eyes the day he won the race.

She loved that man. She had known that first day she saw

him that he was her destiny. Nothing that had happened thus far had changed that. The dance would be the first time they were together in a social situation. Billy would be driving the Brauns' little runabout, leaving Carrie and John alone in her buggy during the ride to and from town. And they would be together for several hours at the dance.

Surely tonight, John would see her as something more than a distasteful job.

eleven

The evening didn't begin as Carrie had hoped. Billy helped Gretchen into their buggy, then, when John made no move to climb down and assist her, he handed Carrie into her buggy.

The sun was setting in a magnificent blaze of color when they followed Billy onto the main road.

"It was thoughtful of the Grange to wait until Jed and Lucille were settled in their new home before throwing this party for them. Don't you think?"

He didn't reply or give any indication he was aware of her presence, despite the fact that her arm brushed against his every time the buggy swayed.

"Gretchen looks really pretty tonight, doesn't she?" Carrie paused long enough for him to answer. When he didn't, she chattered on. "She's wearing the dress she wore to Lucille's wedding." She smoothed down her light green dress. "So am I."

When he still didn't answer, she turned her head away from him.

He stole a furtive glance at her. The setting sun washed over her, transforming her into a red-gold vision. Her dangling earrings captured the light and released it in dazzling prisms of color. Her dress had a scooped neck that revealed just enough golden-touched skin to be intriguing. Her upswept hair was a glory of red-gold curls. The tendrils that escaped and curled on the back of her slender neck caught his attention. There was something about those wispy curls that moved him as nothing else had. He realized his thoughts were taking him to a place he couldn't afford to go, and he forced his attention back to the road ahead.

When they pulled in next to Billy and Gretchen's buggy at the hitching rail, John jumped down and walked around to the horse's head. He expected Carrie to climb down as usual; when she didn't, he started around to help her.

Before he reached her, a handsome young man walked up to the buggy. "Carrie, I thought this was your buggy." He reached up and lifted her down. "I've been watching for you."

"Jake, I'm so happy to see you." Carrie wore a syrupy sweet smile as she spoke.

"You're not with anyone, are you?"

"I am now." John saw Carrie throw a quick glance his way. "Feel free to enjoy yourself, Mr. Thornton. I'll let you know when I'm ready to go."

When she took Jake's arm, Billy, who had been standing to one side with Gretchen, gave John a puzzled look. Then, the two couples walked across the dirt street to the brightly lit Grange Hall.

Jealousy seared through John like a white-hot brand. For a moment, he considered going up the street to the saloon and waiting until she was ready to go. But he didn't. He had never been a drinking man, and didn't enjoy being around men who were. So he squared his shoulders and marched across to the Grange.

He hung his hat on the rack then stood inside the door for a moment scanning the crowd. He had no trouble spotting Carrie. She was talking to another couple—the guests of honor he presumed. She looked up at the young man at her side and made some comment. He laughed and put his arm around her shoulders in a brief hug.

John felt a light touch on his arm and looked down into a pair of laughing blue eyes. "I'm Becky Colton. My friends dared me to come over and introduce myself." She turned and waved saucily to a group of giggling girls, then looked back up at him. "I haven't seen you before. Are you new in town?"

John smiled. "I've been out at the Circle C for a couple of months."

The fiddler took his place on a raised platform and began to warm up for the first set of the square dance. "Would you care to dance, Miss Colton?"

If his smile didn't reach his eyes, she seemed not to notice. "Why, Sir, I don't even know your name." She fluttered her long, dark lashes at him.

"My name is John. Now, would you care to be my partner?"

"I would be delighted to, John."

He caught a brief glimpse of Carrie's flaming hair as he guided Becky across the room.

Even though Becky was small, pretty, and a good dance partner, he had only intended to dance one dance with her. However, she did not allow him opportunity to escape, and he'd lost sight of Carrie in the crowded room by the third dance.

When he finally did spot her, he couldn't believe his eyes. She seemed to be having a wonderful evening without him. As the night wore on, he saw Carrie dancing with several different men. However, the young man she called Jake was obviously monopolizing her time.

Watching Carrie partner with yet another apparently unattached man, he excused himself from Becky and tried to dance with several other women as well. When he saw Jake escort her to the dance floor for yet another dance, John could no longer pretend to enjoy himself. He excused himself from his latest dance partner and went outside. Leaning against the buggy, he nursed his smoldering jealousy. Finally, he stalked back into the Grange Hall.

Carrie was at the refreshment table with Jake. He crossed the room to them.

When she saw John heading their way, Carrie's heart skipped a beat. He was easily the most attractive man in the room. She turned back to Jake, forcing a laugh at the joke he had just told.

"Miss Butler." Carrie turned and looked up at John. There was fire in his blue eyes. "I'm takin' you home."

She wanted to reach out and brush back the wayward lock of hair that lay on his deeply tanned forehead. "I'm not ready to go home, Mr. Thornton."

"I didn't ask you if you were ready, Miss Butler. Get your things together and tell your little friend good-bye. We're leavin'."

"Just a minute, Carrie." Jake put a restraining hand on her arm. "If your driver wants to go, I'll be happy to take you home after the party is over."

Carrie hesitated, and John snapped. "Miss Butler came with me and she's leavin' with me."

"It's my understanding you were hired to be Miss Butler's driver," Jake said. "I think you're a bit out of line, Fella."

John's fists clenched at his sides. "Would you like to step outside and settle this, Kid?"

Jake looked John up and down, assessing the breadth of his shoulders and the strength in his muscular arms and chest. He shook his head. "You're bigger than I am and you have probably done a lot more fighting. I'd be a fool to go up against you." He tightened his grip on Carrie's arm. "But you don't have to go with him, Carrie. He's only a hired man, and I will see you home."

Carrie was aware they were quickly becoming the center of attention. "It's all right, Jake; I'll go with Mr. Thornton."

Jake shrugged. "It's your decision. I'll walk you to your buggy."

The crowd parted as they passed through, followed by John.

Billy intercepted them at the door. "John, if you could spare a minute, I need to jaw at you."

Jake and Carrie walked across to the buggy, and he lifted her into the seat.

"Carrie," Jake took her hand in his. "You know I've loved you ever since first grade. I was wondering if I could come calling on you."

"Oh, Jake! I love you, too, but I'm not in love with you. I never could be. I'm sorry."

Jake released her hand, and shrugged. "Well, you can't blame a fella for trying." He dug the toe of his boot in the dust, then looked up at her. "You're sweet on Thornton, aren't you?"

Carrie blushed. "Was I that transparent?"

"Couldn't keep your eyes off him." He chuckled. "Well, I see him coming so I guess I'd better be going before he pounds me into mincemeat." He started to walk away, then turned back and said, "By the way, I think he's a little sweet on you, too, Carrie."

The two men met in the middle of the street, nodded stiffly, and walked on.

John climbed in beside Carrie and picked up the reins. A stony silence settled over the two occupants of the buggy as he backed out and turned toward the Circle C.

They were almost to the ranch when John pulled the buggy to the side of the road. They sat for a time before Carrie turned her head and looked at him. He was staring straight ahead, but in the light of the full moon she could see a muscle in his jaw jumping. She knew he was angry—though she didn't know exactly why—and she clasped her hands in her lap.

"Well, if you have something to say you might as well say it," she said.

He continued to stare straight ahead. "I guess you know you made quite a spectacle of yourself tonight."

She felt the first small prick of anger. "What's that supposed to mean?"

He turned to face her, resting his arm on the back of the seat. "You know very well what I mean. You flirted outrageously with Andy. That poor little kid would jump off a mountain if he thought it would impress you."

She felt her face growing warm. "Andy is just a kid. I danced with him once. What's really bothering you, Mr. Thornton?"

"All right. You asked. I'll tell you." He leaned toward her. "You flaunted yourself like a cheap saloon girl."

"I flaunted. . ." He was being so unfair. The anger rose in her, choking off her words.

"You hung all over that kid Jake, and he couldn't keep his hands off you."

"Jake is my friend."

"Well, I was almost forced into beating your friend into a bloody pulp to defend your honor."

"My honor! My honor!" Carrie spluttered. "My honor was never in need of defending, Mr. Thornton. Besides, what was I supposed to do? Stand in the corner and watch you dance with every unattached female under the age of a hundred? Except me. You never once asked me to be your partner."

"It was my understanding I was being paid to escort you, Miss Butler. I didn't realize my duties included being your lover as well."

Anger washed over Carrie in a blinding wave. She raised her hand and he caught it before it connected with his face. His other arm slipped around her shoulders and he pulled her to him. Then he did what he had wanted to do since the first time he saw her.

Carrie had never been kissed before, yet instinctively her lips responded to his. Her arms slipped up around his neck and she melted against him.

John didn't know what he had expected. But not this.

Never this. He broke off their kiss and pulled her head down on his shoulder. "Caroline. Caroline." He whispered the words. "My sweet Caroline."

"I love you, John." The words, muffled against his neck came clearly, bringing him to his senses.

He put his hands on her shoulders and held her away from him. "Is that what you wanted, Miss Butler?" he said mockingly. "Well, you can't say John Thornton doesn't do his job."

Her face went dead white and she slapped him hard across the cheek. "Take me home!"

"The lady's wish is my command." He picked up the reins and the buggy once more moved down the road. "But, then, I reckon I just proved that."

As soon as the buggy rolled to a stop, Carrie scrambled down and ran into the house. John drove into the barn. He sat for a time, his head bowed, his cheek stinging, his heart aching. Finally, his movements stiff and mechanical, he climbed slowly down, unhitched the buggy, and put the horse in a stall.

Then, feet dragging, he walked to the bunkhouse.

twelve

Spring roundup began the Monday morning following the party. Long before daylight, Mac pulled himself up on the seat of the chuck wagon, picked up the reins, and headed out. Carrie, riding Brandy, and Andy, on a steel gray cow pony he called Sidewinder, rode alongside the wagon. A wrangler followed with a remuda of two hundred horses.

Half asleep, Carrie slumped in the saddle. She had always looked forward to the roundup, but this year if she could have found a reason to beg off—short of telling her father the truth—she wouldn't have come. She had always thought tears were a sign of weakness, but Saturday night she had cried herself to sleep.

Her spiritual life had been sketchy these last few weeks to say the least. Now, with nowhere else to turn, she prayed, *Father give me strength to face John, and hold my head up after what happened Saturday night. And, please, Lord, don't let me cry when I see him.*

The sun was just coming up when Mac hollered, "Whoa," and the covered chuck wagon came to a rattling halt. "Reckon we'll set up here fer now," he said.

Andy unhitched the horses. Then, he and Carrie turned them, along with Brandy and Sidewinder, out to graze with the remuda.

Mac and Andy began to set up camp.

"What can I do to help?" Carrie asked.

"I figured you'd be goin' out to hunt strays like you always done." Mac looked at her from beneath grizzled brows.

Carrie shook her head. She didn't want to take the chance of running into John Thornton. "Not this time. I thought I'd hang around camp and help you."

"Wal, I reckon while me an' Andy's settin' up, you kin grab one a them baskets an' gather up some cow chips."

Carrie wrinkled her nose. "I'll do that, Miss Carrie," Andy offered.

"No, I'll do it. You help Mac."

The task wasn't really all that bad since she had on gloves and the chips were dry. When the basket was full, Andy helped her carry it back to camp.

One of the Circle C beeves had been butchered to supply meat for the round-up. Mac made a pot of Sonofagun stew and hung it on a tripod over the fire. "Don't never boil it," he said. "Jist let it simmer nice and slow fer two or three hours."

Cooking was easier than Carrie had imagined. "What do we do next?"

"I'd reckon I'll mix us up a mess of sourdough biscuits."

"Let me do it," Carrie said.

"Mebbe you'd best watch me make a batch afore you attempt it yoreself, little lady." Mac climbed into the wagon and Carrie followed. The inside was outfitted with cabinets where food, dishes, and supplies were stored. A baking table was on one side and, across from it, the narrow cot where Carrie slept.

Mac measured potato water into a bowl, then stirred in flour and sugar. "We'll jist set thet aside to rise," he said. "When it doubles, we'll finish up our biscuits."

By the time the first gathering of bawling cattle were driven into a milling circle several hundred feet from the chuck wagon, the meal was nearing completion. Mac had added salt, pepper, and hot sauce to the stew, along with small pieces of chopped sweetbreads and brains. The biscuits were in the Dutch oven. A large pot of coffee hung over the glowing embers.

Limping a few feet from the wagon, Mac banged a large spoon against the bottom of a dishpan. "Come an' get it!" he bellowed, setting off an immediate horse race from the holding grounds.

The men jostled and exchanged good-natured insults as they gathered around the washbasins Mac and Andy had set out for them. After they washed the dirt from their faces and hands, they formed a ragged line.

While all this was going on, Mac and Andy set up a long table. Tin pie pans and cutlery were stacked at one end so that they were within easy reach of the men. Next was the large pot of stew, then a pan of biscuits, and lastly the pot of coffee flanked by large tin cups.

Cyrus stepped to the head of the line. When he removed his hat, the men became silent, pulled off their own hats, and bowed their heads. After Cyrus prayed, he joined Carrie's father at the end of the line. The men slapped their hats back on as they started to move down the serving line.

Mac ladled stew into their plates, Carrie added a couple of biscuits, and Andy filled the cups.

After the last plate was filled, Carrie looked toward the milling herd and saw John. When some of the men saddled fresh mounts and headed back to work, she knew the men riding watch would be coming in to eat. She quickly filled her plate and climbed into the chuck wagon.

After she finished eating, she lay down on the cot. She only intended to rest a few minutes, but when she woke, the branding for that day was over and it was almost suppertime.

Supper that night was roast beef and brown gravy with quartered potatoes that had cooked alongside the meat in the rich broth. Carrie once more took her place between Mac and Andy to serve the biscuits that were left from the noon meal. John went through somewhere near the middle of the line.

His blue eyes captured hers and held her captive for a heartbeat—before she managed to look away. Billy, who was behind him, clapped a big hand on John's shoulder. "That was some mighty fine ropin' you was doin' today."

"This was just a good day."

"You ever do any of the fancy stuff? Fig'r eights and such."

"I know a few tricks, but all a man needs to know is the head and heel catch." John picked up a cup of coffee. "Where I come from, if a man tried anything more than that on the job he might as well pack up his gear."

"Yeah, it'll get you fired here too, but sometimes we like to do a little showin' off after work. Wanna show us what you can do later?"

Carrie's hands were trembling by the time the two men

walked away and she didn't hear John's reply.

Andy, standing beside her pouring coffee, said, "I bet I can do something Mr. Thornton can't."

"I doubt there's anything Mr. Thornton can't do."

"He can't do what I can, Miss Carrie," Andy boasted. "Me and Sidewinder can do somethin' nobody else can."

"And what can you do?" Carrie wasn't really interested, but the men who had gone through the line earlier had been teasing Andy about being a cook. They had called him a grease belly and wanted to know when he was going to be grown enough to do a real man's work. The boy seemed so eager to impress her she felt sorry for him.

"I get way back. Then I run up behind Sidewinder and jump on. Old Sidewinder takes off like a scared jackrabbit and runs somethin' fierce. Want me to show you?"

Carrie shook her head. "I don't want you to do that trick, Andy. It's too dangerous. If you should miss and fall your horse could kick your brains out."

The boy laughed. "Shucks, Miss Carrie, I ain't gonna fall. There's a trick to it, you see. I tie a knot in Sidewinder's tail. I just put my foot on the knot and jump right on."

"That's even worse. If you should slip you could be dragged. Promise me you won't ever do that trick again, Andy."

Andy didn't promise, but when he didn't mention it again, Carrie forgot about it.

By Friday, the roundup had moved to the banks of a shallow creek in the far corner of the Circle C. After breakfast, while the men were out making the morning gather, Carrie walked down to the creek with a bar of soap, a towel, and a blanket. Screened by a stand of cottonwoods, she stripped down to her sleeveless, knee-length, cotton knit union suit, and gingerly stepped into the cold water. She waded slowly out to the deepest spot, which was only a little more than chest high, and lathered up. She swam for awhile, rinsing off the soap, then washed her hair.

When she waded out of the water she felt clean and refreshed. She dried her hair then wrapped the towel around her head. Holding the blanket around her, she gathered up her clothes. When she got back to the wagon, she put on clean clothes from the skin out and hung the wet union suit and her towel on a line inside the wagon to dry. After combing and braiding her damp hair, she climbed out of the wagon to join Mac and Andy as they put the finishing touches on dinner.

Early that afternoon, the last of the herd was branded, castrated, had their ears notched, and were released. With the hard work of the roundup ended, the men trooped down to the creek, as Carrie had done earlier, to scrub a week's worth of dirt and sweat from their aching bodies.

Early Saturday morning, they would head back to the ranch, but the rest of Friday was theirs to enjoy. When they returned from their baths they were clean-scrubbed, dressed in fresh clothes and ready for fun.

They immediately convened a kangaroo court and began to try some of the cowboys for various crimes. No matter how eloquently the accused man argued his case, he knew he was going to be found guilty. The penalties were mainly harmless nonsense, carried out amidst laughter and cat-calls. Finally, a young cowboy called out, "I accuse John

Thornton of bein' too good at ever' thin' he does."

"Guilty," the man acting as judge called out, not giving John the opportunity to defend himself. "What'll his punishment be?"

"We got it right over yonder," one of the men called out, pointing to a wild-eyed steer staked out a short distance from camp. "Saved that killer 'specially fer ol' John. I'm thinkin' he can't stay on thet feller's back fer more than five seconds."

Carrie had been standing with her father, Cyrus, and Mac, enjoying the tomfoolery. Now her eyes grew wide. "Don't let him do it," she said. "Please, Papa! Cyrus! You've got to stop him."

"Looks like we can't do anything about it," her father said. John, surrounded by a group of men, was already striding toward the red-eyed, snorting animal.

"If he didn't think he could handle it, he wouldn't attempt it," Cyrus said. "John's a good man. I'd reckon he's got sense enough not to try somethin' he don't think he can do."

Carrie had spent the past week avoiding the tall, good-looking cowboy. After the mean, hurtful things he had said to her Saturday night, she had told herself she hated him. Now, watching the other men hold the wild-eyed steer immobile with their ropes while he prepared to lower himself onto its back, she knew she could never hate him. She would love John Thornton until she took her dying breath.

The men released the steer and beat a hasty retreat. Carrie watched in horrified silence as the crazed animal used every move in the book to rid himself of the man on his back. When it seemed he had exhausted his bag of tricks, he lowered his head and bucked his hind legs into the air. Close to doing a complete somersault, he suddenly corkscrewed his massive body.

Carrie clapped a hand over her mouth to stifle a scream when she saw John slipping toward the wildly pitching steer's head. Knowing he was going to be impaled on the wicked-looking, razor sharp horns, she squeezed her eyes shut and turned her face against her father's chest.

His arms closed around her. She felt the steady thudding of his heart. Then, a mighty groaning roar went up from the men.

thirteen

The shout became a cheer.

"He's all right, Carrie," her father said.

She opened her eyes and turned to look. Miraculously, John had regained his seat.

Cyrus held a stopwatch in his hand counting off the seconds.

It seemed to Carrie that John had been clinging to the back of the steer for an eternity before Cyrus said, "Five seconds." However, the hand of the watch indicated ten seconds, before John threw his leg over the steer's back and slid off. He landed running. The steer chased him several feet before tossing its head and trotting away. All the men, including her father and Cyrus, rushed forward to crowd around John. Feeling as though her bones had turned to water, Carrie sank to her knees and wrapped her arms tightly around herself. Her head dropped forward and she could feel tears running down her cheeks.

"You all right, little lady?"

She felt a gentle touch on her shoulder. Lifting her head, she looked into Mac's worried eyes. "Oh, Mac! Why do I have to feel like this?"

"I'd reckon not even old Solomon with all his wisdom could answer thet question, little lady."

"He said such cruel hurting things to me, but it's as

though ever since the first time I saw him I've known him. The real him, not the face he shows the world, but the kind, gentle man he is inside."

"I know, little lady. I know." He reached a hand down to her. "Here, let me help you up from there."

She took his hand and scrambled to her feet. "Were you ever in love, Mac?"

"I wuz, an' still am. I reckon I'll allus love Emily."

Carrie had never thought that Mac might have had a life before she knew him. A life she knew nothing about. "What happened?"

"She died of the cholera durin' the war. Her and our little baby boy." He pulled a red bandanna from his pocket and blew his nose.

Tears filled Carrie's eyes. "Oh, Mac, I'm so sorry."

"Now don't you go gettin' all weepy on my account." He stuffed the bandanna in his hip pocket, and cleared his throat. "It wuz a long time ago, an' I reckon I'll be seein' 'em agin afore long."

Carrie wiped her tears away on the sleeve of her shirt. "Were you ever sorry, Mac? Did you ever wish you'd married someone else? I mean since Emily died."

"Nope. Fer some of us they's only one love, little lady."

"I know I'll never love anyone else."

Mac reached out and patted her arm. "In thet case, I wish I could tell you jist to foller your heart. But, I cain't, little lady. I jist cain't."

❧

Since Mac wanted to get as much packing done as possible that evening, supper was served early. Carrie stood between

Mac and Andy putting corn bread on plates heaped high with Cowboy Beans. There had been a couple of horse races after the kangaroo court, but all the men could talk about was John's ride. Billy and John were together near the middle of the line. Carrie smiled at Billy. "Congratulations on your race. That Cayuse can really run."

He smiled. "Thank you, Miss Carrie, but compared to what John here done, the race was small potatoes. Did ya see him ride?"

"I saw him," Carrie said, noncommittally.

"What did you think of my ride?" It was the first sentence he had spoken to her since Saturday night, and she supposed she should have been thrilled, but. . .

"I stayed on double my time."

There was something in his manner that seemed so cocky—so utterly male—he infuriated her. He had frightened her half to death. Now he was standing here preening before her like a peacock. Did he expect her to flutter her eyelashes and tell him how wonderful he was?

"Was that intentional?" She plopped a piece of cornbread on his plate. "I thought you just didn't know how to get off."

Before he had a chance to reply, she snapped, "You're holding up the line. Move on!"

Mac chuckled. "Thet's tellin' 'im, little lady."

Andy said softly, "You wasn't very nice to Mr. Thornton, Miss Carrie."

"Mr. Thornton hasn't been very nice to me."

"But he's a hero."

"Hero." Carrie snorted. "I thought you knew the difference

between a hero and an idiot. Mac and Cyrus are heroes. They fought in the Civil War. There wasn't anything heroic about what John Thornton did today. It was foolhardy and show-offish, and I wasn't impressed."

"In my book, any man that can stay on the back of a buckin' steer, with jist a rope to hang on to, is a hero. Just wait till you see my trick with Sidewinder."

"I told you to forget that stupid horse trick. In the first place, you can't do it. In the second place, if you try, you're likely to get your neck broken. And, in the third place, I don't care." She slammed a piece of cornbread on the last plate, then tore her apron off. "Grow up, Andy!" She stalked away.

"I don't care what Miss Carrie says, when I do my horse trick the men'll quit callin' me grease belly."

"There ain't nothin' wrong with bein' a cook. Ever'body knows an outfit travels on its belly. Besides, life's a precious gift God gives to us," Mac said. "An' the little lady's right. Real heroes don't risk their life 'less they's a good reason fer 'em to do so." He handed Andy a plate. "Now come on an' eat. We got a heap a dishes to warsh tonight, an' I don't reckon the little lady'll be back till she's cooled off some."

౭

The dishes were done and packed away when Carrie joined Mac and her father beside the chuck wagon. Billy and John were performing a series of fancy moves with their lariats. Approximately twenty-five feet separated the mounted men as they faced each other, matching trick for trick. What they were doing was more an exhibition than a contest, and Carrie settled down next to Mac to watch. She didn't even miss Andy until he called out her name. "Watch me, Miss Carrie!"

She turned her head and saw Sidewinder. Andy, his bare feet throwing up little puffs of dust, was already running toward the horse. She clutched Mac's arm, and they both started up. Before they had time to call out, Andy jumped. His foot slipped through the knot and kicked the horse's rump. Startled, Sidewinder leaped forward. While they watched in horrified silence, the frightened horse ran toward the opening between John's and Billy's horses, dragging the struggling boy with him.

Two lariats shot out. Both loops settled around the runaway's neck. He ran another twenty feet or so before the loops tightened, bringing him to a stop. The two men had already made a few dallies around the saddle horn, now they locked the rope with a half hitch and dismounted.

Carrie ran to Andy and knelt to put her arms around the frightened boy. "Oh, Andy, you could have been killed."

John, who had been sawing through the horse's tail with his knife, freed the boy's foot before turning on Carrie. "This was all done for your benefit. Anyone with any sense would have discouraged him from tryin' such a dangerous stunt. But you egged him on, and you almost got him killed."

"I didn't. . ." Carrie started to protest, then jumped up and pushed through the men gathered around Andy.

When her father started after her, Mac put a restraining hand on his arm. "Let 'er go, Sherman. The little lady needs to be alone, an' I'm a-goin' to have a little talk with young Mr. Thornton."

John was helping Andy to his feet. Mac hobbled over to him. "Somebody else will take care of the boy. You an' me is a'goin' to have us a little confab."

Billy stepped in to help Andy, and John followed Mac in the opposite direction Carrie had gone. Away from the creek.

⁊ֵ

As soon as she was out of sight of the men, Carrie began to run. She ran until her chest ached. Then she made her way slowly to the bank of the creek, sat down on a fallen log, and buried her face in her hands. Tears stung the back of her eyelids and she blinked them away. Carrie had spent so much time alone, she had become accustomed to speaking aloud to herself. "You will not cry, Caroline Abigail Butler! Tears never solved anything," she said sternly. "Do you hear me?"

She began to pray softly to herself, begging God for his guidance. She remembered Gretchen's mother telling her that she couldn't force John to love her. Then, she recalled something she had overheard Cyrus tell one of the wranglers last summer.

Cyrus had been quite a gambler before his conversion twelve years ago and he sometimes used the gambler's vernacular when making a point. The man had been having trouble reaching a decision concerning some land he had a chance to buy. Cyrus had advised, "Well, Cole, it's like this—you've got to study the situation real close. If you think you got a good hand, stay in. But, if your cards is bad, you'd best just throw them down and get out of the game." Cole had evidently been holding a winning hand; he had his own little ranch now.

Carrie lifted her head and looked out at the water. "You don't have even one good card, Carrie Butler," she said softly. "It's time you threw down your hand and got out of the game."

The sun was just sinking beneath the horizon when John found Carrie. Her back was slumped and he knew she was crying. Guilt washed over him. Mac had given him a good dressing down and he had deserved every word the fiery little man said. He walked around the end of the log and stood, hat in hand. "I've been lookin' for you," he said.

She glanced up at him. She wasn't crying. But there was a guarded, watchful expression in her dark eyes.

"Andy's scraped and bruised some, but he'll be all right." He hesitated a moment. "Mind if I sit?"

She shrugged and turned her face back to the creek.

He sat down a couple of feet from her and looked down at the hat he was twisting in his hands. "I owe you an apology," he said, darting a quick glance at her. She hadn't moved.

His gaze moved to the creek. "I'm sorry for the things I said to you back there. I thought, well, I knew the kid was sweet on you, and I reckon I thought. . ."

Because he had been showing off for her, he had assumed the boy was, too. But that wasn't something he could admit. Not even to himself. "Andy told me you warned him not to try that stunt, but he thought the men would be impressed."

She still didn't move.

"I want you to know I'm sorry for what I said the night of the party. There was nothin' wrong with the way you behaved. I was just. . ." He couldn't tell her he had been jealous. No more than he could admit he'd stayed on the back of that Idaho brainstorm longer than was necessary because he knew she was watching.

"All I can do is ask your forgiveness, Caroline. Miss Butler. I'm truly sorry, and I'm ashamed of the way I behaved."

She turned her head and looked gravely into his blue eyes. "You're forgiven, Mr. Thornton." She stood up and brushed her dark riding skirt. "But I want you to know one thing. Men who risk their lives for no reason do not impress me. Men like Papa and Cyrus and Mac are my heroes."

She turned and walked hurriedly away.

A bullfrog boomed, calling for his mate. A distant warble answered the nearby trill of a mockingbird. A fish leaped to catch an errant dragonfly skimming over the surface of the water, then splashed back into the creek. John Thornton sat alone in the gathering darkness.

fourteen

The Monday after they returned from the roundup, John and Carrie resumed their daily rides. By the beginning of the second week, everything appeared to be as it had been before, but John sensed a wariness in her. A holding back.

He tried to convince himself this was what he wanted.

He had come to Kansas to execute Sherman Butler. His resolve was no less than it had been.

In the quiet loneliness of the night, he told himself that he had already lingered too long. He needed to complete his mission and move on.

The next morning when he rode beside Carrie over the gently rolling prairie, the hot dry wind rustled through the tall thirsty grass. The passage of their horses flushed a covey of quail. The startled birds skimmed across the prairie with a whir of wings.

Carrie turned to him with a delighted smile, and his heart whispered, *How can I leave her?*

"If I had been carryin' a shotgun we would have had quail for supper," he said.

"Oh, no!" Carrie's soft brown eyes widened. "They still have young ones. Mamas shouldn't be taken away from their children."

He smiled. "They're only birds."

"Even little birds need their mamas. Do you have a mother, John?"

He looked away from her. "Not anymore."

She couldn't see his eyes, but she saw the set to his jaw. "You miss her, don't you?"

He shrugged. "Sometimes."

She dared one more question. "Are you an only child?"

He glanced at her. "I had a younger brother, but he died."

She saw the curtain descending over his blue eyes. "I had an older brother," she said, "but I never knew him. He died before I was born."

He didn't reply. This brief glimpse of John Thornton's past was all she could expect today.

She turned Brandy toward the Nolan place. "I want to see about the apples," she said. "Besides, it's so dry I know the flowers on the grave need water."

Carrie walked beside him from the well to the grave, and stood quietly while he poured the water slowly over the cracked earth.

"I wasn't quite eight when Mama died," she said. "She was mostly in bed the last year, and I don't remember her very well, but I know she loved flowers."

He lifted the bucket over the fence. "That should take care of them for today."

She nodded. "We'll have to come every day and water them."

They walked slowly back to the well. Carrie pushed her soft tan Stetson back and let it dangle by the chin strap. She raised her face to the cloudless blue sky. The wind snatched at the loose strands of hair that had escaped her braid and now blew them across her face. "Cyrus says we're ripe for a fire," she said.

John pushed his hat to the back of his head and scanned the horizon. "It's dry enough for sure," he said. "And the way that wind's blowin'. . ."

He left the sentence unfinished as he lowered the bucket into the well. He pulled it up, filled to the brim, and set it on the well curbing.

"Would you like a drink?"

He picked the bucket up and held it for her while she drank deeply. She wiped her mouth with the back of her hand while he drank. When he sat the bucket back down, she dipped her cupped hand in and splashed the cool water over her flushed face and neck.

Watching her, he smiled. She looked up and saw the gentle expression in his blue eyes. *I've known him forever,* she thought.

To cover her confusion, she turned and walked to Brandy. Slipping her foot into the stirrup, she swung herself into the saddle. He mounted Jet and they turned back toward the ranch.

They hadn't ridden far when she said, "Mama loved Papa enough to die for him."

He looked sharply at her. She blushed. "I have a habit of talking to myself."

She reached a gloved hand down and patted Brandy's neck. "I was thinking about something Mac told me the other day."

"I wouldn't think that was something Mac would talk about."

She straightened up in the saddle. "Real men do use the word love, Mr. Thornton.

He felt her moving away from him. Closing him out. "No, that isn't what I meant. I just. . ."

She turned in the saddle to face him. "Mr. Thornton, I told you after the roundup that I wasn't impressed by showy bravado. Now, I'm going to tell you what I do admire."

They reined in their horses. John hooked his leg over the saddle horn and turned enough to see her face while she talked. She sat straight-backed. Prim. Proper. Ladylike. Her eyes straight ahead. "Mama was a descendant of Sam Houston on her father's side," she said. "And the Spanish conquistadors on her mother's side. She was born to wealth and privilege." She shot a sidelong glance at him and saw his quick grin. "That is the way Mac said it," she defended.

She relaxed, and turned to face him. "I'm not sure how they met—Papa says he was just an ordinary cowpoke— but they fell in love. Her family didn't approve of him from the beginning, but Mac says Mama was strong-willed. They finally agreed to let them marry, but when she insisted on following Papa to Kansas they disinherited her. Mac says she was like fine china. Fragile and easily broken. But, Mac says, that didn't stop her. She came here with Papa and she worked right alongside him and Cyrus and Mac to build this place to what it is today. Mac says when Mama knew she was going to die, she told him she would rather have had fifteen years with Papa than a lifetime in a fine mansion with any other man. Mac told me that Mama knew when she left Texas she wasn't strong enough for life on the frontier. He says she knew she was facing a death sentence when she came here, but still, she loved Papa enough to die for him."

John knew how hard life could be for women who left comfortable homes to follow their men into uncharted territory. He supposed there was an element of truth in the story the old man told Carrie. But why would any woman follow a cold-blooded killer like—

"Mama died a few days before my eighth birthday." Carrie's soft voice called his attention back to her. "Papa grieved something terrible. I felt like I'd lost both of them for awhile."

He saw remembered sorrow in her soft brown eyes. "Mac and Cyrus stepped in. After Papa got well, the three of them raised me. They washed my face and combed my hair. They sat beside my bed when I was sick. They scolded me when I misbehaved. Not one of them was ever afraid to say the word love."

She looked down at her hands, which rested lightly on the reins. "They did something else. They taught me that the Bible is the inspired Word of God. They told me that the Old Testament shows us where sin leads. The New Testament shows us the way out of sin. They taught me that the teachings of the New Testament are to be our guidebook for this life. I have never known Mac, or Cyrus, or Papa to compromise their Christian beliefs."

She raised her eyes to him and he saw tears clinging like dewdrops to her long, dark lashes. "I gave my heart to Jesus Christ when I was twelve years old. I promised He would always be the Master of my life. That's something I seem to have forgotten these last few months."

She took up the reins. "We'd best be getting home."

He dropped his leg down and kicked his foot into the stirrup. They rode slowly and silently across the prairie. The ranch house was in sight before she spoke again. "Mac and Cyrus have done their best to take Mama's place, and I love them and Papa with my whole heart. But sometimes I'm so lonely."

He didn't reply, but she hadn't expected him to. She urged Brandy forward.

John dropped a few paces behind. Watching her slender, straight back and the swinging auburn braid of her hair, he felt his heart swell and crowd up into his throat. He wished there was some way to spare her the pain to come, but he knew there wasn't. Tomorrow, or the next day, or some day very soon, he was going to finish what he had come here to do, and Carrie would be faced with a new sorrow.

They rubbed the horses down in silence. When they came out of the barn, Carrie said, "I won't be riding in the morning. Gretchen is spending the night and we have plans for tomorrow."

He watched her walk away, then went to the corral and selected a fresh mount. A few minutes later he rode out.

The next morning John rode the fences checking for breaks. He was thinking about Carrie when he topped a slight rise and saw a rider in the valley below him. He recognized the big man astride the Appaloosa. Reining in, he slipped from the saddle, and led Jet into a copse of scrub oak. He slid the Winchester from its scabbard and flipped up the calibrated sight.

The man dismounted and knelt to examine something on the ground. Butler's broad back was to him. John lifted the rifle to his shoulder and sighted down the barrel. There was no way he could miss.

Carrie's face appeared between him and her father's back. "I love Papa with my whole heart," she said.

He lowered the gun and shook his head to clear it. He once more lifted the rifle to his shoulder. "I've been so lonely," Carrie's soft voice said inside his head.

Again, he lowered the rifle. Then, for a third time he raised it to his shoulder. Butler's back was still turned to him. All he had to do was pull the trigger. Still he hesitated.

He'd killed men before. But not like this. He'd never shot an unarmed man. Always before they had been facing him. They'd gone for their guns first. No matter how vile their crime, they'd had a chance. He had walked away because he was faster than they were.

He lowered the rifle. He couldn't kill Butler like this. He wanted him to know why he was dying.

He took the few steps to Jet and slipped the rifle back in the scabbard. He put his foot in the stirrup and swung into the saddle. As he turned Jet away from Butler, he saw a wall of smoke rising in the southwest. Driven by the wind, it was moving swiftly across the prairie in their direction.

John broke out in a cold sweat and his heart began to pound. He fought the urge to run. To put as much distance as possible between himself and the fire. Butler was still in the valley. He turned back and urged Jet down the rise toward the big man.

fifteen

By the time the two men reached the ranch house to sound a warning, then raced to the fire, the greedy flames had crossed the barbed wire southern boundary of the Circle C and were moving fast.

The crew from the Circle C were joined by the Brauns and their hands, as well as the men from several surrounding ranches. Buckboards from the various ranches, carrying barrels of water, were pulled up and left at a safe distance from the fire. Between fifty and seventy-five men spread out along the northeast perimeter of the fire, beating at the flames with wet gunny sacks.

Carrie helped Mac fill the barrels of water in their buckboard, then rode out with him. After Mac parked a safe distance from the fire, they both climbed down to join the line of men. They no sooner got the fire stamped out in one spot than the wind urged it to life somewhere else.

When Carrie ran back to the wagon to dip her sack in water, she searched the line of soot-blackened men for John. But she didn't see him.

Meanwhile, John was several hundred feet away fighting the fire, as well as a much more formidable adversary. He had faced danger most of his life. Few things frightened John Thornton, but fire terrified him.

John turned to go back to the wagon and found himself

facing a wall of crackling flames. He turned to his left and flames shot above his head. He turned to his right. More flames. A sudden shift of wind had sent the fire back on itself, trapping him in the center of a blazing inferno. A circle of death.

An agonizing scream tore from his throat, as he ran blindly back and forth searching for a way out. He imagined he could smell his hair singeing, was positive he could hear the sound of his skin beginning to fry like fat bacon in a hot skillet. Blind panic seized him. He screamed again and again.

Suddenly a huge, shapeless figure burst through the fire. Steam rose from it and he knew Death had come for him. It reached out for him. Doubling his fists he backed away. Something crashed into his chin. Then there was only blackness.

John struggled to escape the darkness. Slowly, inch by painful inch, he pulled himself up out of the inky black pit, and forced his eyes open. Carrie was bending over him. Her face was pale and smudged with black. He wanted to wipe the soot from her face but he hadn't the strength to life his hand.

"I love you, Caroline." The words were a painful croak.

She smiled and he felt her hand on his hair. He struggled to stay awake, but he was so tired. Slowly his eyes closed.

"I love you, too." He heard her softly spoken words, as he began the slow spiral back into the darkness.

❧

When he next woke, he was lying between clean sheets in

a shadowy room. He heard water running and turned his head toward the sound. Rain was streaming down the windowpane. His throat hurt and his tongue felt as if it were glued to the roof of his mouth.

A strong arm slipped around his shoulders and lifted him to a sitting position. The rim of a cool glass touched his cracked lips. Ignoring the soreness of his throat, he drank greedily. "More!" he demanded hoarsely.

The arm lowered him back onto the pillow and the glass was taken away. "Not just yet," a man's voice said.

John's eyes were adjusting to the dim light and he could make out Sherman Butler's features, as the big man bent over him. "Where. . .?" His throat hurt when he tried to talk and he couldn't complete the sentence.

"You're at the main house. We brought you here so we could look after you. You gave us a scare, but you're going to be fine. You swallowed quite a bit of smoke, so your throat may be sore for awhile. And, your lips are cracked some from the heat."

"The little lady smeared so much ointment on you thet you look like you oughta be entered in a greased pig contest." Mac appeared beside Butler, and looked down at John. "You'll be jist as purty as ever in a couple a days, but right now, yore a mite blistered."

John wondered where Carrie was. He raised his hand to the gold chain around his neck. His hand moved down over his bare chest to his waist. He was wearing some sort of light trousers. He felt clean, and knew someone must have bathed him. Surely, she hadn't been in the room when they put him in bed.

"Afore Sherm sacks out, you want us to help you take a little walk, air would you ruther use the commode?"

John shook his head. "No! No commode."

Mac chuckled. "I thought not. They's an outside door here. If'n we hurry you won't even get damp."

The cool, damp air felt good on John's face and chest, but he was glad to be back in bed. Butler left, and Mac lit a lamp and settled down in the circle of light with a book.

John lay looking at the ceiling and trying to remember what had happened after he was trapped. A man—for now that the panic was gone he knew it had been a man wrapped in a wet blanket—had braved the flames to rescue him. It must have been Billy. He raised a hand to explore his jaw and winced. Old Billy packed quite a wallop.

"Yore jaw's a mite sore, ain't it?" Mac chuckled. John moved his head so he could see the old man. His book lay open on his lap. His faded blue eyes twinkled as he regarded John over the top of the wire-rimmed spectacles perched on the end of his nose. "Sherm's got a right like the kick of a mule, don't he?"

John frowned. It had been Butler that carried him to safety? He turned his face to the wall. Slowly the darkness closed around him once more.

It was still raining when he woke again, but it was daylight. Carrie stood beside the bed looking down at him. He yanked the sheet up to his chin, and she laughed. "Who do you think put you to bed yesterday afternoon, Mr. Thornton?"

She laughed again. A light, happy laugh. "You can relax. They wouldn't let me see you until you had Papa's pajama trousers on and were all tucked in. Ready for some breakfast? I brought you a tray."

He suddenly realized he was ravenous, and, clutching the sheet around his neck, pushed himself up against the pillows.

She set a lap tray across his legs. "However, I did rub ointment all over your chest and face, Mr. Thornton." She winked. "In my opinion, you haven't got a thing to be ashamed of."

She took a napkin off the tray and shook it out. "Would you like me to feed you?"

He scowled. She smiled and handed him the napkin. He remembered opening his eyes yesterday and seeing her bending over him. Her face, beneath the soot and dirt, had been pale and frightened, but she hadn't cried. He recalled thinking how much he loved her. Surely, he hadn't spoken the words aloud.

"I've already had my breakfast so I'll sit over here in the chair while you eat. If you want anything, let me know."

He grunted and picked up his fork. The eggs were perfect, the bacon was cooked to a turn, the gravy was thick and creamy, and the biscuits were so light, they seemed to float from the plate. He washed the meal down with a pitcher of cold milk. When he was finished, he wiped his mouth with the napkin and lay back against the pillows. When she came to take the tray, he ventured, "Did you cook breakfast?" and was pleased to find he was only slightly hoarse.

A startled expression crossed her face, then she shook her head. "No, Mac did."

He managed a teasing grin despite his sore lips, "I'd ask Mac to marry me if he wasn't so ugly."

"I don't think he's exactly what you'd want in a wife, Mr. Thornton."

"I'd reckon you're right, Miss Butler. But, pretty faces are easy to come by. A good cook, on the other hand, is a priceless jewel. My mother used to make the best Southern Pecan Pie and her apple pies would melt in your mouth."

Carrie gazed thoughtfully at him, then she picked up the tray and left the room.

It continued to rain, but several of the men stopped in, one or two at a time, to visit him. None of them stayed longer than five minutes, and John told Billy he was beginning to feel like a malingerer, lying in bed while the other men worked. Billy laughed and said none of them were doing anything much because of the weather. He should just enjoy the rest and the nice soft bed while he could.

He hadn't seen Carrie since breakfast, and now it was almost noon. When Butler came in to check on him, he said she was involved in some secret project in the kitchen. John wondered what she could possibly be doing that would keep her occupied all morning. When she brought him his noontime meal, he noticed a smudge of flour on her nose.

"Here's your dinner," she said, setting the tray across his lap, and handing him his napkin.

She perched on the edge of the bed watching him put away a huge rib-eye steak, and a heap of golden-brown fried potatoes. As soon as he was finished, she took the tray.

"I made you something special for dessert," she said, and left.

When she came back, she was carrying a huge slice of apple pie on a small plate. She handed him the pie and a fork before once more sitting down on the edge of the bed.

John looked at the pie. It didn't look like his mother's. Hers always had a neat fluted edge. This one didn't really have an edge. It looked a little bit as though she had stood back and thrown the top crust on. He suppressed a smile at the mental image. At least the crust was nicely browned. He looked from the pie to Carrie. She was watching him with an expectant smile. "I made it as a surprise for you," she said.

He smiled at her, then poked a forkful of pie in his mouth. He was surprised all right. She must have used salt instead of sugar. He grabbed the glass of water from the table beside the bed and swallowed it in one gulp. "More!" he gasped.

Carrie picked up his fork. He shook his head and thrust the glass in her hand. She took a tiny nibble of the pie and handed him the water pitcher. While he drained the pitcher, she put the pie on the bedside table, then buried her face in her hands.

He returned the empty pitcher to the table. She was still sitting with her face hidden by her hands, but he could see her shoulders shaking. His heart ached for her. She'd worked so hard, and she had done it for him.

He put his hand on her shoulder. "Don't cry, Darlin'! I don't care that you can't cook. I still like you better than Mac."

She dropped her hands from her face and turned to him. "Well, I should hope so," she chortled. He pulled her into his arms. They hugged each other, and laughed until tears streamed down their faces.

After their laughter died away, Carrie remained in his arms, leaning against his chest. Her hand reached out to toy with the locket suspended from the heavy gold chain around his neck. "This is beautiful. Where did you get it?"

"It belonged to my mother. My father gave it to her on their wedding day." His arms tightened around her for a heartbeat, then he released her.

She sat up to examine the locket more closely. It was an intricately engraved two-by-three-inch oval. He took it from her and pressed a hidden spring, then handed it back to her open. "This is my Ma and Pa."

sixteen

Carrie studied the images in the locket. The dark-haired young man was wearing the uniform of the Confederacy. The girl's hair was light, and she was very pretty. "You look like your father," she said softly.

Finally, she handed the locket back to him. He snapped it closed. "A picture of Mama in her wedding dress hangs above the fireplace," she said. "I'd like for you to see it sometime."

He didn't reply. She looked at him and saw that his eyes were closed. She leaned over and kissed him gently on the lips, then scooted off the bed. She brushed the lock of hair back from his forehead. "Sweet dreams," she whispered, and tiptoed quietly from the room.

When John heard the door close behind her, he opened his eyes. What was he going to do? His sole purpose in coming to Kansas had been to avenge the death of his family. Hatred for the man who killed Ma and Pa, and stole Lucas's life, had driven him for twelve years. Now, he was lying in his enemy's bed, sheltered by his roof, wearing his pajamas.

Worse yet, he was in love with the daughter of the man who had murdered his family. What was he going to do? He squeezed his eyes shut and two tears rolled slowly down his cheeks. "What should I do, Pa?"

He saw in his mind his father and mother sitting at the kitchen table. Pa's Bible lay open before him.

Pa read aloud. " 'But I say unto you, Love your enemies, bless them that curse you, do good to them that hate you, and pray for them which despitefully use you, and persecute you.' "

Pa reached a hand out to Ma. "Mavis, we must pray for Sherman Butler and these other men. They are wanderin' lost through life, tryin' to avenge somethin' that's been over for fifteen years." He reached his other hand out to Lucas. "Come, pray with us, Son. And, I want you to remember one thing, Lucas. Vengeance is a circle. If you let it, it'll just go on from generation to generation destroyin' endlessly. Someone's gotta break the circle, Son."

They had joined hands around the table and prayed for the salvation of their enemies. That night, Sherman Butler had come with his men. His gentle, peace-loving pa had died. And, Ma. And, Lucas had been destroyed, too.

Where had God been when his family was being slaughtered? While his family lay in the ground, Sherman Butler had grown powerful and rich. Where had God been the last twelve years? God had told Cain the voice of his brother's blood cried out to Him from the ground. Surely, the innocent blood of his family had a voice. Cain had been punished for his crime. Sherman Butler had prospered. It wasn't just. If God wasn't going to punish Butler, then he had to.

The vision of Carrie's beautiful face interposed itself on the back of his eyelids. He blinked his eyes open. His feelings for Butler's beautiful red-haired daughter went far beyond mere physical desire. He had known other women. But always he had been able to leave them and ride away without a backward glance.

Carrie was different. His feeling for her went far beyond the attraction he had felt when he first met her. He loved her. The kind of love that called for a visit to a preacher, and led to a home and children. 'Til death do us part love. The kind of love his parents had shared.

His hand went to the locket lying against his heart. He could no longer deny his love for Carrie. But no matter what the cost, his family's murderer must pay for their deaths. He had to finish what Sherman Butler had started twelve years ago.

The next day it quit raining. John moved back to the bunkhouse and returned to work.

One morning Carrie and John rode out to look at the damage from the fire. Already new grass was pushing up through the black stubble of the burned off pasture. "Isn't it wonderful how nature renews itself?" she asked.

He nodded in agreement, but his eyes were on her. Carrie had always been beautiful, but since the fire, she was incandescent. He knew he was responsible for the glow that emanated from her, and while he told himself it would be better if she didn't love him, some basic instinct buried deep in him was proud that she could love him so much.

"I want to show you something," she said, and turned Brandy toward the creek.

They rode for some time before they entered a grove of trees. Carrie reined Brandy in and slid from the saddle. John dismounted and moved to her side. She reached out and took his hand. "This is my secret place," she said. "I've never told anyone about it, not even Gretchen and Lucille. I come here when I'm sad or lonely. I never wanted to share it with anyone before, but I want to share it with you."

Her brown eyes were innocent and soft with love. John knew she was offering a very special part of herself to him. He also knew he wasn't worthy of her trust. He should turn and walk away. His fingers closed around her hand. Side by side they walked through the trees.

The Garden of Eden couldn't have been more beautiful than Carrie's secret place.

She looked up at him. He slipped his arm around her waist, and pulled her close. His heart pounded in his ears, drowning out the sound of the waterfall, as he bent his head to her. The kiss they shared beside the serene little pool spoke of a lifetime of loneliness and yearning. When he released her, she lay her open hand against the side of his face, then smoothed back the curl of golden-brown hair that dropped over his forehead. He traced the line of her soft, full lips with a gentle fingertip as he memorized every feature of her face.

Neither of them spoke when they once more joined hands and walked back to their horses.

❧

As soon as they rode into the ranch yard, they noticed a crowd had gathered at the side of the smaller corral, where the horses were broken. They caught a glimpse of a man lying on the ground.

"It's Papa!" Carrie jumped from Brandy and ran toward the corral. She was already kneeling on the ground beside her father when John walked up and joined the other men.

He moved over to stand by Billy. "What happened?"

Billy turned a worried face in his direction. "He was breakin' a bronc and that sidewinder run him into the fence. His leg's broke, but Cyrus thinks it's a clean break. Mac went to the house fer a blanket. They sent Abel to town after the Doc. Soon as Mac gits back we're gonna carry him in the house."

When Billy turned to say something to the man on the other side of him, John looked at the man on the ground. Butler was at least two inches taller than John's six feet two inches, and easily weighed two hundred fifty pounds. Not an ounce of it fat. Sherman Butler was a big, muscular man. A powerhouse of a man. And, looking at him lying helpless on the ground, John realized that he was still a young man. Just into his forties, he reckoned, and not really looking even that.

Carrie smoothed the thick auburn hair back from her father's forehead. "Does it hurt terribly, Papa?"

"Nah!" he said. "But, I'm getting old, little girl. Five years ago something like this wouldn't have happened."

"You're not old," she protested. The men parted, and she looked up. "Here's Mac now. They're going to carry you inside and put you to bed."

Carrie scrambled to her feet and stepped back while Mac spread the blanket out beside her father. The men lifted him as gently as possible and laid him on the blanket. He didn't make a sound, but his face paled, and beads of sweat broke out on his forehead. John knew it must have hurt terribly, and admitted a grudging admiration for the big man.

Carrie walked beside the improvised stretcher, holding her father's hand, while they carried him to the house. The other men trailed along behind and John went with them.

They laid him on the big bed in his room, blanket and all. Cyrus took a knife and slit the left leg of his denims. An ugly red and purple bruise discolored the leg from the knee down. They pulled the boot from his right foot. Then Cyrus flicked open the knife and moved to his left foot.

"What do you think yer a-doin'?" Mac growled.

"I'm cuttin' his boot off." Cyrus scowled. "What's it look like I'm doin'?"

"Well, what's he s'posed to do with only one boot?" Mac demanded.

"I don't know, Mr. McDougal, I reckon you jist might have to dig into your cookie jar and buy him a new pair." Cyrus brandished the knife while the two elderly men argued.

Butler raised up on his elbow, "Am I going to have to get out of this bed and whip both of you?" he thundered.

"I jist don't see no use a-ruinin' a perfectly good pair of boots," Mac grumbled.

"Well, what do you want me to do, jist yank it off him?" Cyrus shouted, waving the knife around his head like a saber.

"Forevermore!" Carrie's voice rose above the men's. "Cut that boot off before his leg swells up and you can't get it off."

While they yelled at one another, John saw something he hadn't allowed himself to see before. These four people—the sweet gentle girl he loved, her father, and the two crusty old cowpokes—were a family. He didn't know how Butler and the two older men had come together in the first place, but he had no doubt of one thing. The four of them were bound by something stronger than blood. In spite of all the yelling—or perhaps because of it—it was plain to see how deeply they loved one another.

He turned and walked out of the house. Jet and Brandy were still where they had left them. He took Brandy in the barn and rubbed her down. Then he mounted Jet and rode toward the west.

It was twilight when he came back to the ranch. Billy was standing by the corral when he turned Jet in with the other horses. He leaned against the fence beside him.

"How'd it go?"

"Carrie stayed right at her pa's side while the Doc set his leg. He'll be laid up awhile, but he'll be good as new when the leg heals."

John glanced at the other man. "How'd she take it?"

"Carrie?" Billy shrugged his shoulders. "She done fine. Carrie's a strong little gal. By the way, she said she wanted to see you when you got home. She's waitin' fer you in the house."

John thought about refusing, but he wanted to see that she really was all right. He turned on his heel and walked to the house.

He found Carrie in the spacious main room. She was sitting on a large, leather-covered couch and looking up at the portrait that hung over the massive rock fireplace.

He hesitated at the door and she turned her gaze towards him, then rose, and crossed the room to stand in front of him. She slipped her arms around his waist, as if it were the most natural thing in the world to do, and rested her head against his chest. Instinctively, his arms went around her, and he held her close.

seventeen

She stepped back and took his hand. "I'm glad you're here."

"How is he?"

"The doctor gave him laudanum for the pain and he's asleep. Come, sit with me for awhile." She urged him toward the deep leather couch.

John quickly glanced at the open beams above his head. The rough cream-colored stucco walls. The massive sandstones that framed the large fireplace and soared to the roof peak. The bookcases that filled most of one wall.

He had been in the parlors of a few rich folks, and this was nothing like those rooms. There was no silk, or satin, or brocade here. No delicate furniture a man was afraid to sit on for fear he'd break it. Instead, the massive couches and chairs were deep, inviting, and covered in leather. Woven wool rugs with Indian designs were scattered over the polished hardwood floors. Those fancy parlors looked cheap and tawdry compared to this.

They sat down on the couch. "This is Mama," she said. "Wasn't she beautiful?"

John looked up at the woman in the portrait. "She was very beautiful," he said. And she was. But not nearly as beautiful as Carrie.

With a contented sigh, she snuggled against him. He put his arm around her and she rested her head on his shoulder.

There was comfort in their silence. Finally, she said, "I miss her so much, John. Today when I saw Papa on the ground, I was so scared. I don't know if I could bear to lose him, too." Her hand was toying with a button on the front of his shirt. "I'm so glad you are here with me. I've been so lonely, John. So. . .very. . .very. . ." Her hand dropped away from his shirt.

He saw that she had fallen asleep. He eased her down and covered her with a blanket that was folded over the arm of the couch. Then he stood and looked at her. Her long dark lashes shadowed her flushed cheeks. Her soft, full lips were slightly parted. She looked young, innocent, and terribly vulnerable. Tears stung the back of his eyelids. Blinking them back, he slipped quietly from the room.

John didn't see much of Carrie the remainder of that week; she devoted all her time to caring for her father. He hadn't expected her to go to church on Sunday morning, but when the Circle C wranglers rode out, she was in the buggy beside Mac. Cyrus trailed along behind with the other men.

John watched them drive down the long lane before he went back to the deserted bunkhouse to gather his things. Then, he strapped on his gun belt, and walked slowly to the house. He slipped through the kitchen door and walked carefully down the hall to Sherman Butler's bedroom.

Butler was propped up against the pillows asleep. John eased into the big chair across from the bed.

He sat for half an hour, trying not to think about Carrie, before Butler stirred and opened his eyes. He gave a little start when he saw John, then smiled a greeting. "I thought

I was alone," he said. "What can I do for you, John? Or did you come to visit?"

John rose and walked slowly across to stand beside the bed. He looked directly into the big man's eyes. "My name is not John Thornton," he said, "and I have come here to kill you."

"I don't understand." The man's eyes were questioning, but there was no fear in them. "Who are you? Why do you want to kill me?"

"My name is Lucas Nolan. On the night of August 21, 1880, you murdered my mother and my father."

"Lucas?" Butler's eyes searched his face. "Lucas was killed with his parents. Is this some sort of hoax?"

Lucas reached up and pulled the locket to the outside of his shirt. "Have you seen this before?"

Butler nodded. "I saw it when we put you to bed the day of the fire."

Lucas flipped a switch and the locket sprang open. He held it where Butler could see the pictures inside. "This is my mother and father. She was standing in front of the window when you came with your men. A defenseless woman. A sweet, gentle woman who never hurt anyone." He fought against the tears he felt crowding into his throat. "She was clearing the supper dishes from the table when you killed her. The house was already burning when Pa put her locket around my neck. He boosted me out the window and told me to run. I waited until you shot him then I ran. Now, I'm back. And, you're going to pay for what you did."

Lucas snapped the locket shut and dropped it back inside his shirt.

Butler shook his head. "Thank God you're alive," he

said. Then he buried his face in his hands and wept.

Lucas shifted from one foot to the other, unsure of what to do next. He had been prepared for Butler to beg for his life. He hadn't expected this.

Finally, the big man lifted his head. "Cyrus always said you weren't there, but I thought he was wrong. I didn't see how you could have escaped." Before Lucas realized what he was doing Butler reached out and grasped his hand. "I didn't kill your parents, Lucas. But I was at least partially responsible for their deaths. Please, sit down. Let me tell you what happened that night."

Lucas's eyes never left the big man's face as he sank slowly down on the bed at his side. What he had to say wouldn't change anything, but Butler had the right to defend himself.

"Your father fought in the Confederate Army. My father was a Union soldier. I know that doesn't seem like a reason to hate a man. But I hated anyone who fought on the side of the South. When you moved here, I wanted you out. I didn't personally cut your fences, or foul your water hole, or run off your stock. But some of the men from nearby ranches did. And I looked the other way."

He leaned forward. "You must understand, Lucas, Kansas was solidly behind the North during the war. There were a lot of old Jayhawkers still around. Men who thought John Brown was a hero. August 21 was a Saturday night. A bunch of good-for-nothings had gathered at the saloon in town. They got a few drinks in them—they weren't the most sterling characters at best—and six of them decided to burn your folks out."

"You were there," Lucas interrupted. "I saw you."

"I was there. We all three were. Me. Cyrus. Mac. One of the men that worked for us was at the saloon. He rode out here and told us what was happening. We got our men together and rode over there as fast as we could. We were too late to save your folks, but the six drifters were still there. Then several of the other ranchers showed up."

He passed a hand across his eyes. "There was no doubt they were guilty. We hanged all six of them in that big tree."

"Caroline told me she didn't know why it was called the hanging tree."

"She doesn't. Mac has always thought we should tell her about the hangings, but I never wanted her to know. I was afraid she wouldn't understand."

Lucas knew Sherman Butler was telling the truth. Everything he had believed the past twelve years was a lie. Half his life he had hated an innocent man. He struggled to his feet. "I'm sorry."

"Don't be. I understand, Lucas. More than you will ever know, I understand."

"I'll be goin' now." He turned at the door. "Tell Caroline—" He shook his head. "Never mind. It isn't important."

"Don't leave, Lucas!" Sherman reached out a beseeching hand. "Your folks' place belongs to you. Please stay."

"No!" Lucas said harshly. Then his voice softened. "I can't."

He turned his back on Sherman Butler's pleas and walked away.

❧

Lucas was tying his bedroll on behind the saddle when

Carrie and Mac drove into the ranch yard, followed by Cyrus on horseback.

Carrie jumped down from the buggy and ran to him. "John, where are you going?"

He finished securing the bedroll before turning to face her. She was wearing something pink. His heart ached until he thought it would burst. "I'm leaving."

"Leaving?" She clutched at his arm. "You can't leave me. Please! Don't leave me, John."

"I have to." He gently removed her clinging fingers from his arm, and held both her hands tightly in his. "There is no John Thornton, Caroline. There never was. It was all a lie. Everything was a lie. I am a lie."

"No!" Tears were streaming down her face. "I love you and I know you love me. That isn't a lie. I love you. It doesn't matter who you are."

"I don't even know who I am, Darlin'." He felt the wetness of his own tears. "I have to find out."

He released her hands and swung into the saddle. "Goodbye, Caroline."

He turned Jet and they galloped away to the west. Carrie ran to the house. She collided with Cyrus coming out the back door. He reached out to steady her. "Your pa told me ever'thing. Don't worry, Young'un. It's goin' to be all right."

He patted her arm, then hurried to his horse, mounted up, and followed Lucas.

Carrie flung herself on her bed. Her mother's Bible was lying beside her. She clutched it to her, and sobbed until there were no tears left. Finally, she lay quiet and exhausted. "If you were here, Mama, what would you tell me?"

There was no answer. "You didn't let anything keep you from Papa," Carrie whispered. "I'll go after him. I'll follow him to the ends of the earth if I must, but I won't let him go. I'll never let him go."

She pushed herself into a sitting position. When she laid the Bible on the bed beside her, the cream-colored envelope fell out. She opened it, took out the card, and read the words her mother had written. *"To every thing there is a season, and a time to every purpose under the heaven."*

She returned the card to the envelope. On a whim, she opened the Bible to the place her mother had marked with the frayed ribbon marker. At the beginning of the third chapter of Ecclesiastes, she saw the words her mother had written on the card. She read the first eight verses. Then read them again. Suddenly what Mama had been trying to tell her was crystal clear.

"Not my will, but Thine," she whispered. "Oh, Lord, forgive me. I've been a headstrong selfish fool. Lord, take my life. From this day forth I belong completely to You."

She lay for several minutes praying and crying. Prayers of surrender and submission. Tears of repentance and joy. With recommitment came renewal, and a deep peace engulfed her.

She got up from the bed, straightened her clothes, washed her face, and smoothed her hair.

Mac tapped on her door. "Air you all right, little lady?"

"I'm fine," she said, and knew that she was now. "I'm just fine, Mac."

"Wal, yer pa and me got somethin' to tell you if you feel like talkin'."

She glanced at her mother's Bible lying on the bed. "Thank you, Mama," she whispered.

She opened the door and kissed Mac's worried face. Then she linked her arm in his, and they walked down the hall to her father's room.

eighteen

Lucas walked through the orchard, stepped over the low fence, and knelt beside his parents' grave. Only one perfect red rose still bloomed on the bush he had transplanted when he first came to the Circle C.

"The last rose of summer," he murmured. The lines of the old Thomas Moore poem came to his mind. He snapped the rose from its life-giving stem and scattered the petals over the grave. " 'When true hearts lie withered, and fond ones are flown, Oh! who would inhabit this bleak world alone?' "

"You don't have to be alone, Lucas."

He started, and jumped quickly to his feet, his hand on the gun at his side. When he saw who it was, he relaxed. "That's a good way to get yourself shot, Cyrus."

Cyrus chuckled. "Yeah, I reckon it is. I had better sense than to walk up behind a man with a gun in my younger days. Reckon I'm gettin' careless in my old age."

Lucas stepped over the fence. "What're you doin' here?"

"Sherman sent me because he can't come hisself. He wants you to stay."

Lucas shook his head. "Didn't he tell you I came here to kill him?" he asked, and started to walk away.

Cyrus followed him through the orchard. "Yep! He told me you was aimin' on shootin' him, but you never could."

"You don't know how close I came the day of the fire." Lucas caught up Jet's reins. "I had him right in my sights. It was just luck I didn't kill him."

"Maybe." Cyrus nodded. "But more likely it was the grace of God stayed your hand."

"You can call it whatever you want. All I know is, I came here seekin' justice for Ma and Pa. You all took care of that twelve years ago. Now it's time I was movin' on."

"Is that what you really want, to jist keep movin' from place to place. Driftin' until you meet someone that can draw faster or shoot straighter. Is that the way you want your life to end, Lucas? Layin' dead in some dusty street with no one to care. I left a little girl cryin' her eyes out—"

"I don't want to talk about her," Lucas interrupted. "Leave Caroline out of this."

"You can't leave her out." Cyrus pulled on his ear. "Do you think when Carrie finds out what brung you here, she'll quit carin' about you? Cause if that's what you're thinkin', you don't know our Carrie very good."

"It isn't just that." Lucas put one foot in the stirrup to mount. "Everything I am was shaped by my hatred for Sherman Butler. I trained for the day I would come back to face him, just as a soldier trains to do battle. I thought about little else. And it was all a lie. Somewhere between the hatred and the lies, Lucas Nolan was lost. I don't know who I am any more. Butler told me this morning that he understood. But he doesn't. Nobody does." He swung into the saddle. "Until I know the truth, I have nothing to offer Caroline."

Cyrus put a hand on Jet's bridle. "Sherman said he told

you everything, but I reckon he didn't."

Lucas's eyes narrowed. "What do you mean? Did he have more to do with my folks' killing than he said?"

"No, he told you straight enough about what happened here, I reckon." Cyrus pulled on his ear lobe. "I'm talkin' about what happened before that. Sherman weren't old enough to fight in the war. Ain't you a mite curious about how come he hated the rebs so much he didn't even want your pa livin' close by?"

Butler had said he hated the Confederacy. It hadn't even occurred to Lucas, until now, to wonder why. He stepped down from Jet. With Cyrus leading the way the two men walked over and sat down on the sandstone foundation.

Cyrus began to talk. "Me and Mac was with Sherman's father during the war. Jim was a good man. He got killed at Shiloh. Before he died, he asked me and Mac to see about his wife and boy. We promised him we would. It was three of the longest, most miserable years you can imagine before the war ended, but we kept our promise."

His eyes took on a far away look as he peered into the past. Lucas waited impatiently for him to continue.

"We found the place right off," Cyrus said. "The house was powerful in need of paint. But the fields was plowed, and things looked to be well cared fer. We couldn't raise nobody, so we jist set down on the porch and waited. Along about twilight, this tall, gangly, redheaded kid comes in with a team of mules hitched to a plow. We knowed soon as we seen him he was Jim's boy. He was surprised to see us, but when we told him we was friends of his pa, he invited us to stay fer supper. He told us Abigail—that was his ma—had died some time ago. He didn't tell us how she died. Not until later."

"How old was Mr. Butler?" John asked.

"He wasn't more than fourteen, just a young'un, and all alone. I didn't have no kin to speak of, and Mac's wife and little boy had died with cholera durin' the war. We kinda threw in with the kid and we stayed there fer a year or so." Cyrus kicked at the hard-packed earth with the toe of his boot.

"To make a long story short, the boy was restless and so was we. He sold the farm fer what he could get—which was precious little—and we commenced to roam. We finally ended up in Texas, which was no place fer a young'un with a grudge agin the South, which is what Sherman was. He hated Johnny Rebs worse than anyone I ever seen. You see the war was over fer me and Mac. We jist wanted to fergit it. But it hadn't ended fer Sherman. One night he told us why."

Cyrus paused in his narrative to collect his thoughts before he continued.

"Seems Abigail had been at the house alone when a bunch of Reb foragers come along. They violated her and they tortured her, then they stole everything they could carry, and they left. When Sherman come in from the field that evenin' he found his ma. She was still alive, but they wasn't nothin' he could do fer her. She died that night. Sherman buried his ma, but he never buried his hate fer the men that killed her. It festered and grew inside him fer six years. Then we come to Texas. He was eighteen years old, and he wasn't a skinny kid no more;

he was full-grown. Texas had been on the side of the South. She was crawlin' with Johnny Rebs itchin' fer a fight. Sherman never started a fight, but he never backed down from one neither."

John looked at the other man, "So, Mr. Butler was a gunfighter?"

Cyrus nodded. "I reckon you could say that. He's good with a gun, Lucas. Real good. Best I ever saw, and I seen plenty. He got quite a reputation. Then he met Miss Caroline Houston. The gunfighter and the lady. They fell in love. Her folks wasn't what you'd call real happy about the match, but Caroline had a mind of her own. They had a big, fancy wedding. I reckon the Houstons thought they could break Sherman to lead, and make an acceptable son-in-law out of him. When they found out they couldn't, they tried to get Caroline to leave him and come home."

"Carrie said her mother loved her father enough to die for him," John said.

Cyrus' face grew thoughtful. "That she did." Then he chuckled. "Caroline had spunk. She stayed with Sherman." He pulled on his earlobe. "Sherman fergot about hatin' Johnny Rebs fer awhile. He begin to work real hard at providin' fer his family. I reckon he didn't want Caroline to think she'd made a mistake stayin' with him instead of movin' back into that big mansion with her folks. After the war, there was a lot of cattle roamin' free. They didn't wear no brand, and nobody wanted them, so we rounded us up a good-sized herd. We waited until Caroline had Matthew, then, soon as we knowed everything was all right, we trailed them cows to Kansas. Like I said, Sherman had quite a reputation in Texas; now that he was a family man, he thought it might be best not to go back. There was plenty of land here. So we decided to stay. Soon as we got a cabin built, Sherman went fer Caroline and the baby."

"So that's the story?" Lucas asked.

"Not quite," Cyrus shifted a bit on the stone they were sitting on. "I ain't told you the most important part yet.

"Caroline was a Christian and soon as the church was built her and Mac—he'd been a believer since he was a young'un—started goin' to church. She gentled Sherman down some, but she never could git him to go to church with her. Then your folks moved in, and the hate in him flared up again. Oh, he never done nothin' to hurt your pa directly, but we sat by while other folks did. Then they was killed.

"My shame at what we'd done—or more rightly what we hadn't done—drove me to my knees. But not Sherman. The guilt gnawed at him somethin' awful, but he hardened his heart. Then Caroline got sick. He never let hisself believe she'd die. When she did, he pushed everybody away, even little Carrie, and closed the pain up inside."

John felt a sharp pain for the small girl he barely remembered. "It must have been a difficult time for Carrie."

Cyrus nodded. "Yes. It was a hard time for all of us. Anyway, to get back to my story. Finally, Sherman took a Bible and a jug of water and went to one of the line shacks. I was afraid he'd harm hisself and I wanted to go after him. Mac said no. He said the time had come fer Sherman to make a decision. He said we'd be a heap more help stayin' home prayin' than we would followin' and interferin' in the

Lord's work. I was kinda new at the prayin' business, but Mac weren't. So, that's what we done." Cyrus drew a deep breath before he continued.

"There'd always been a lost look in Sherman's eyes, even before Caroline died, but when he come home that look was gone. We knew then that he'd found what he'd been searchin' fer."

When Cyrus fell silent, Lucas stood up. "Thanks for telling me, Cyrus. My pa said vengeance was a circle, and I reckon he was right."

"It's a circle only as long as nobody steps out. But, that's what you done today, Lucas. You stepped out. The circle of vengeance is broken. There's a place for you here. Carrie loves you, and I'm askin' you to stay."

"I can't." He turned and walked to where Jet was grazing, and Cyrus followed. He picked up the reins. "For the first twelve years of my life I was Lucas Nolan. For the last twelve I've been John Thornton. Half my life I've carried a load of hate inside me. Now the hatred is gone and there's a big empty space where it was. I feel like an empty shell, Cyrus. I have nothin' to offer Carrie."

"I reckon we're all empty shells, Son, until we meet the Lord."

"Don't you understand, Cyrus? Carrie doesn't know Lucas Nolan. She knows John Thornton. And, John Thornton never existed. The whole last twelve years has been a lie." He put his foot in the stirrup and swung into the saddle.

Cyrus put a hand on the younger man's knee. "Do you think you're the only man that's ever changed his name?

Sherman Butler never existed until twenty years ago. I told you he was a gunfighter when we was in Texas. He had a different name then, Lucas. If I was to tell you what it was, you'd recognize it jist like you recognize the name of Bat Masterson, or Wyatt Earp, or Doc Holliday, or Wild Bill Hickock, or any one of a dozen others that lived by the gun. Sherman wasn't that different from you, Son. In many ways you put me in mind of him."

Lucas leaned over the saddle horn and looked down at the older man. "There's somethin' I want you to know, Cyrus. I was never a gunfighter. The first eight years I was on my own, I did what I had to do to survive. Mostly muckin' stables, and then later, when I was old enough, wranglin'. I tried never to do anything that would shame the memory of my pa and ma. The last four years, I was a Texas Ranger."

Cyrus brushed an invisible mist from his eyes. "I know your folks would be right proud of you, Lucas."

"I like to think so." Lucas blinked the haze from his own eyes.

Cyrus cleared his throat. "Well, like I wuz sayin', when we come here, he wanted a new start, so he took a new name. But, changin' names don't change a man, Son. It was what happened in that line shack eight years ago that changed Sherman.

"I see that same lost look in your eyes as I used to see in his, and as I used to see in my own when I looked in the lookin' glass. We all got that empty space you was talkin' about, Lucas. Don't none of us really know who we are 'til we let the Lord fill us with his love and forgiveness. Your ma and pa was Christian folks. They'd want you to follow their lead, Boy."

Lucas looked out over the vast, beckoning prairie. "I know they would, Cyrus. And, maybe someday I will. But, right now, I can't."

The older man sighed, "Well, I reckon I understand how you feel, Lucas. But one of these days the Lord's gonna speak to you, Boy. When he does, don't you run from Him."

"I've got to be on my way." Lucas reached out and the two men shook hands.

"I'll be prayin' fer you, Son. We all will. And when your roamin' days is over. . ." Cyrus squeezed the young man's hand before releasing it. "Jist don't fergit where home is."

Lucas raised his hand in a final farewell, then nudged Jet into a gallop.

Cyrus stood watching until they disappeared from sight. Then he mounted up and headed back to the Circle C.

nineteen

For the next few months, Lucas drifted, never staying in one place more than a few days.

For twelve years, he had allowed himself few friendships and no attachments. It had been a hard, lonely life, but one he deemed necessary, and he had adapted. Now, he felt as barren as the desolate land he rode across and as empty as the vast sky that stretched over his head. Carrie was never far from his thoughts, and the loneliness cut through him like a knife.

He spent the fall in Colorado and Utah. When he woke to find the first snow blowing across his bed, he drifted south to Arizona, then New Mexico, and finally back to Texas.

One morning he woke to the sound of birds singing. The sun was shining and billowy white clouds drifted lazily across an azure sky. It had been almost a year since he rescued Carrie from the runaway buggy. It seemed an eternity since he rode away from her. It was time to move on. That night he gave notice to the foreman, and left the Texas ranch where he had worked the past week.

He wandered aimlessly northwest. It was late afternoon when he rode into a small town in Oklahoma. He tied Jet to the hitching rail in front of the saloon and went inside. Twenty minutes later he came out, untied Jet, and swung into the saddle.

"Well, Boy, looks like we might get us a job at the Bar X. The bartender said they were hiring. We just follow this road five miles. He says we can't miss it."

On the edge of town, a large tent had been set up. Wagons, buggies, and saddled horses crowded the surrounding field.

"Looks like they're havin' themselves a revival meetin'," Lucas said, and started to urge Jet on. Then a familiar tune drifted from the tent, and a woman began to sing.

୧

The day Lucas rode away from her, Carrie left her girlhood behind. She had been led—by the cryptic messages her mother left for her—to read the complete passage from the Bible. In reading it again and again, she had come to understand what her mother was trying to tell her. *"To every thing there is a season, and a time to every purpose under the heaven."* A time to love and a time to let love go.

When her father and Mac told her what had happened at the Nolan place twelve years earlier, she knew why John Thornton had so exactly matched her mystery man. The Mysterious Stranger had been created—not from the fantasies of a lonely young girl—but from her memories of Lucas Nolan. When she was a small girl, she loved twelve-year-old Lucas Nolan. When John Thornton appeared, that love was rekindled.

She had lost Lucas twice. The first time when she was five, and again when she was eighteen. Now, she was nineteen, and she knew Lucas wouldn't be back this time. It had taken much prayer, and a lot of soul-searching, but she had finally accepted that she would spend the rest of her life alone.

Lucille hadn't returned to her position in the small school, and Carrie had offered to fill in. She taught the entire term, and she loved it. Seeing the expression of wonder on young faces when they finally grasped the solution to a difficult problem, or realized for the first time that they were actually reading, had proved fulfilling beyond her expectations. She had always loved children. Since she would never have her own, perhaps God was calling her to teach other people's children.

Now that the school term had ended, she found herself at loose ends. One warm spring day she rode out to her secret place. Leaving Brandy on the edge of the grove of trees, she walked to the pool. The spring rains had swollen the creek and sent the water roaring over the waterfall, before it rushed on its way. Still, the small pool was as peaceful as ever.

Carrie pushed her hat off and let it dangle down her back. Kneeling on the edge of the pool, she leaned forward to examine her face in its placid depths. It was the same face that had looked back at her a year ago, yet there were subtle differences. A new serenity. A peacefulness. A maturing of the girlish features.

Another face appeared above hers in the mirror-smooth waters. A lean, masculine face, with a lock of golden-brown hair falling over the wide forehead, and a slight dimple in the square chin. A face she had thought she would never see again.

She sprang to her feet and flung herself against his broad chest. His arms closed around her. She felt the strong beat of his heart. She lifted her head, and stepped back enough to look at him. Lines of fatigue etched his tanned face. He was dusty from the trail and he needed a shave. She didn't notice those things. They didn't matter.

She searched his eyes, and found what she was seeking in their blue depths. They were no longer John Thornton's cold, hurting eyes. These were the gentle eyes of the boy who had given a small girl the last cookie in the cookie jar. They were Lucas Nolan's eyes.

"You've come home to stay, haven't you?"

"If you still want me I have," he said, and there was a question in his blue eyes.

She raised her face to his. The kiss they shared answered all their questions, and erased the months of loneliness.

๛

Later, they walked slowly along the bank of the creek, leading their horses. She told him about her pupils and Gretchen and Billy's December wedding.

He told her of his life in the months after he left her.

"Always before, I read everything I could get my hands on," he said. "Yet, when I was involved in someone else's life, I forgot how lonely I had been in those days."

Carrie understood. She had whiled away many lonely hours reading. She squeezed his hand in silent understanding.

He returned the gentle pressure of her fingers. "This time all I could think about was you," he said, "and what I had left behind."

"I prayed for you every day," Carrie looked up at him, and her brown eyes glowed. "But I didn't think you'd ever come back to me."

"I had nothing to give you, Caroline."

"You had yourself. That's all I ever wanted, Lucas."

"I couldn't even offer you myself. I was lost." He released her hand and put his arm around her shoulders. "A little over a week ago—in a small town in Oklahoma—I found myself. I'd like to tell you about it."

She slipped her arm around his waist and rested her head against his shoulder. "I'm listening."

"I was lookin' for a job when I passed a big tent. I figured they were havin' a revival—an' I for sure didn't want no part of that—so I started to hurry Jet past. Then, someone began to play the piano and a woman started singing 'Amazing Grace.' " He shot a quick glance at Carrie before he continued.

"When I was a boy, the first thing I heard every morning when I woke up was my mother singing hymns as she fixed breakfast. 'Amazing Grace' was her favorite, and it was always one of the songs she sang."

They stopped walking, and Carrie looked up at his face as he talked. "It was like somethin' was drawin' me to that tent. I thought it wouldn't hurt anything to sit outside and listen 'til she was through singin'. Next thing I knew I was walkin' in. I found a seat in the back and sat down. They sang a few more hymns, then the preacher got up. He was a big strong-lookin' man. Reminded me of your pa." The corners of his eyes crinkled with a smile as he looked at Carrie.

"I remember he took his text from Matthew 18:11–14. But I couldn't tell you what he preached. Somethin' about the lost sheep, I reckon. All I remember is when the sermon was over he gave an invitation. It was like an invisible hand was pulling me forward. Next thing I knew I had taken the sawdust trail, and was kneelin' at the altar in front of everybody, sobbin' my heart out."

Tears were trickling down Carrie's cheeks. He cupped her chin in his hand. "I know who I am now, Darlin'. I'm Lucas John Nolan, a child of the King. I'm not empty anymore, Caroline, but without you, I am incomplete. I still don't have anything in the way of material possessions to offer you; everything I own is tied on Jet's back—"

Carrie interrupted. "I don't care, Lucas, all I ever wanted was—"

He put a silencing finger across her lips. "I'm not finished yet, Darlin'. I've been rehearsin' this speech for hundreds of miles. If you'll let me finish, you can talk all you want. All right?"

She nodded, and he removed his finger. "Now, where was I? Everything I own is tied on Jet's back, except for one thing." He dug down in the watch pocket of his denims and brought out a small velvet bag. He loosened the drawstrings and shook a wide gold band into the palm of his hand. "This was my mother's wedding ring. I know she would be proud to have you wear it."

"Yes," Carrie said.

"Now wait a minute, I haven't asked you yet. I want to do this proper like."

"Of all things, Lucas Nolan! I've been waiting for this day since I was five years old. I don't care anything about proper."

"But I do. I want this to be a day you'll tell our granddaughters about." He dropped to one knee and took her hand in his. "Caroline, I can't offer you much. All I have is myself. But my heart belongs to you, and it always will. Will you be my wife?"

Her face was wet with tears, as she stood looking down into his eyes, but she didn't say anything.

"Well, will you marry me, or not?" Lucas finally demanded impatiently.

She wrinkled her nose. "I'm thinking about it."

"Thinkin' about it! You already said yes." He scrambled to his feet. "You have to marry me, Caroline. I love you. I can't live without you. Without you my life wouldn't be—"

"Now, that's what I consider a proper proposal." She grinned up at him. "Yes, Lucas Nolan, I will marry you. And I will love and honor you all the days of my life."

He frowned at her. "What about obey?"

She gave a saucy toss of her head. "That's negotiable, Mr. Nolan."

twenty

If it had been left up to Carrie, they would have been married the week after Lucas came home. However, Lucas and her father had other plans. When they finally selected the date for their wedding, it seemed far in the future to Carrie. Much, much too far. But there was so much to do, and they were so busy, the months passed swiftly.

Carrie woke before daylight on the first Saturday morning in August. Today was the day. At two o'clock this afternoon, she would become Mrs. Lucas John Nolan. Her mother's wedding dress was hanging in the wardrobe, pressed, and ready for her to wear. Despite her happiness, tears welled up and rolled slowly down her cheeks. If only Mama could be here to see her in the dress she had worn on her own wedding day.

She sat up and lit the lamp on the table beside her bed. Last night, when her father came to tuck her in, they had talked for over an hour. Then, he had taken a familiar cream-colored envelope from his pocket. "Your mother wrote this that last evening." He cleared his throat before he was able to continue. "The next morning she didn't wake up."

He tucked the letter inside the front cover of her mother's Bible. "Caroline asked me to give this to you the night before you were to be married. She wanted you to read it first thing on the morning of your wedding."

When he leaned over to kiss her good night she put her arms around his neck and clung to him. "I love you, Papa, and I'm going to miss you so much."

"I love you, too, little girl." His voice clogged with emotion as he held her close. "But Lucas is a good man, and you're only going to be a few miles away."

They had talked a few more minutes about Lucas, and about the house he had helped Lucas build for her that summer. Then, he had kissed her once more, turned off the light, and left her to her dreams.

Today was her wedding day. The Bible lay in the soft circle of lamplight. She reached out and opened the front cover.

Propped up against the pillows, she studied her mother's spidery script on the face of the envelope. *For my precious Carrie on her wedding day,* she had written. Tears welled up in Carrie's eyes. She brushed them away on the corner of the sheet, and ran a fingernail under the flap of the envelope. The dried glue separated easily. She unfolded the thick sheets of paper and began to read.

My beloved daughter,

her mother had written.

Today is your wedding day.
How happy and excited you must be. And perhaps a little sad also because I cannot be there to see you in my wedding dress. Oh, Carrie, Darling, I do hope you are going to wear my dress. It is such a beautiful dress.

But it doesn't really matter what you wear. Only that you are happy.

By this time, I am certain you have examined the items in the trunk that I left for you. When I had your papa pack them away, I enclosed little notes explaining the significance of each item. Today, I had your papa bring my little lap desk so that I might explain more fully.

The first thing you come across will be my Bible. This is the foundation you must build your new home on, Carrie. If Christ is truly the head of your family, your marriage will be strong and endure.

The second thing will be the tiny handbag I carried to my first dance. It is a symbol of the carefree days of youth.

The third thing is my wedding dress. It signifies the joy of earthly love.

The fourth item is the tiny christening dress both of my babies wore. It represents the miracle of life.

The last item is the lock of hair from Matt's first haircut. It is representative of the uncertainty and sorrow that is a part of every life.

I am ready to make my final journey, Carrie. In these last weeks of my illness, the first eight verses of the third chapter of Ecclesiastes have gained a precious significance for me. I firmly believe there is a season and a time to every purpose under heaven. I have had a wonderful life, Carrie, now it is my time to die. And even though I regret that I must be parted, even temporarily, from you and Sherman, I am eager to join my Savior.

    I want you to know, my darling, that my love encircles you this day and every day of your life.

Love,
Mama

Her mother's last conscious thought had been of her. Tears blurred Carrie's vision as she folded the two sheets of paper and returned them to the envelope. "Thank you, Mama," she said softly. "I do know what you were trying to tell me. I believe I have known ever since the day Lucas went away."

The sky in the east was growing rosy when she slipped the letter between the pages of the Bible. A tap on the door, and Mac's gruff command to get up brought her from her bed.

"We're a-waitin' breakfast on you, little lady," he said. "You'd better be a shakin' a leg if you want yore pa to drive you to Lucille's place. You ain't wantin' to be late fer yore own weddin', air you?"

She was going to get dressed for the wedding at Lucille and Jed's house in town. "I'll be right there, Mac." Carrie pulled her robe on and opened the door. She planted a kiss on Mac's whiskery cheek and linked her arm in his. Together they walked down the hall to the kitchen where Cyrus and her father were waiting.

ⱦ

"Ease off some, Gretchen," Carrie gasped. "You're squashing my innards."

"Hush!" Gretchen ordered, giving a final yank on the

corset's laces. "There, we're done."

"I swore I'd never wear this awful contraption again," Carrie said. "But Mrs. Wright refused to let out any seams."

"You look so slim," Lucille said, hoisting her swollen body from the bedroom chair she had been sitting in. "I don't think I shall ever be slim again."

"Nonsense! Of course you will," Gretchen said. "Except for your belly, you're still skinny as a stick."

Gretchen carefully removed the sheet from Carrie's dress, and caught her breath. "Oh, Carrie! It's the most beautiful dress I've ever seen."

The two young women slipped the dress over Carrie's head, being mindful to not mess her hair, and arranged the full folds of the skirt around her. Then Lucille began the task of fastening the dozens of tiny satin-covered buttons that closed the back of the full-sleeved, scoop-necked bodice.

When she was finally finished, they both stood back and looked at Carrie. "You're beautiful," they breathed in unison.

She had chosen to wear her hair loose, caught back at the sides with silver combs that had belonged to her mother. Auburn curls spilled over her smooth shoulders and cascaded down her back in a copper waterfall to her waist. The friends' three-way hug was somewhat impeded by Lucille's eight-month pregnancy and their care to not muss Carrie's dress.

They laughed as they drew apart. "This is just like a fairy tale," Lucille said. "Who would ever have thought that "The Mysterious Stranger" was Lucas Nolan all along."

"Or that he would practically come back from the dead

to save your life," Gretchen added, her blue eyes shining.

"It's so romantic," Lucille clasped her hands over her bulging belly.

"Now you'll live happily ever after," Gretchen said. "Just like the princesses in the stories."

Carrie shook her head. "If there's one thing I've learned, Gretchen, it's that there's no such thing as happily ever after. Lucas and I will be happy for the most part, but I'm sure we'll have our share of pain and heartache." She glanced at the small clock on Lucille's bedside table. "It's time to go."

As her friends adjusted the folds of her veil, Carrie remembered frail, thin hands stroking her hair. The light flowery fragrance of her mother's perfume still lingered in the dress she wore, and in that moment Carrie felt that her mother was with her.

A tap sounded at the bedroom door, and Lucille opened the door. "It's time, Carrie," her father said.

"I'm ready, Papa." Carrie turned to face him.

Tears came to his eyes. "You look so much like your mother did on our wedding day," he said.

Carrie smiled as she reached out to him. He took her hand in his, and they walked slowly from the bedroom followed by Lucille and Gretchen.

❧

Lucas and Carrie joined hands and he looked into her soft brown eyes as they repeated their vows. She was radiant and his love for her swelled up into his throat.

This evening they would go home to the little house that he and her father had built for her on the foundation of his parents' house. There, on the site of so much tragedy, they would raise their family. The small house would grow as children were born until it became large and sprawling. A swing would hang from the outspread limb of the old tree in the front yard, and the sounds of laughter and childish voices would banish the last memories of the mob violence that had robbed him of his own childhood.

"Do you have the ring?" Had he lost the ring? Lucas felt a moment of panic, then Billy handed the wide gold band to the preacher, and he breathed a sigh of relief.

The preacher held the ring in the palm of his open hand. "I want you to notice that this ring is a perfect circle," he said. "As the circle has no beginning and no ending, so too, the love Caroline and Lucas share is never ending. Lucas, please take the ring and repeat after me, as you place it on Carrie's finger. "I, Lucas, take thee, Caroline. . ."

Carrie's eyes never left his face as Lucas repeated his vows. He was so dear to her. The last few months under Mac's expert tutelage had convinced her she would never be much of a cook, and housekeeping didn't inspire her. She prayed that he would forgive her inadequacies. She so wanted to be a good wife to him.

"With this ring I thee wed," Lucas said. She looked down as he slipped his mother's ring on her finger. It was a perfect fit.

Carrie repeated her vows, promising to love, honor, and obey. Then, feeling a bit inhibited by so many eyes watching, they shared their first kiss as husband and wife.

Carrie's father, looking proud and happy, but a bit teary-eyed, was sitting in the front pew of the packed church.

Mac and Cyrus, wearing new black suits, were seated beside him. Their shirts were dazzling white; their boots polished to a mirror shine. Mac pulled a faded red bandanna from his pocket and wiped his eyes. When he noisily blew his nose, Cyrus scowled at him, then covertly wiped at his own eyes.

The three men followed the newlyweds up the aisle. Lucas opened the door and the five of them stepped out into the bright August sunlight.

"Welcome to the family, Son," Sherman said.

Lucas ignored his new father-in-law's extended hand and threw an arm around his shoulders. Carrie's heart sang with happiness as she watched the two men embrace.

Lucas reached out and drew Carrie and the two older men in. He gazed around the circle of happy faces. The five of them—Carrie, Sherman, Mac, Cyrus, and himself—were a family now.

His father had said vengeance was a circle. But so was love. He looked into his wife's glowing brown eyes, then down at the golden gleam of his mother's ring on her slender finger.

The circle of hate and vengeance had been broken by the most powerful force on earth. Love.

A Letter To Our Readers

Dear Reader:

In order that we might better contribute to your reading enjoyment, we would appreciate your taking a few minutes to respond to the following questions. We welcome your comments and read each form and letter we receive. When completed, please return to the following:

Rebecca Germany, Fiction Editor
Heartsong Presents
PO Box 719
Uhrichsville, Ohio 44683

1. Did you enjoy reading *Circle of Vengeance* by M. J. Conner?
   ❑ Very much! I would like to see more books
      by this author!
   ❑ Moderately. I would have enjoyed it more if

   _____

   _____

   _____

2. Are you a member of **Heartsong Presents**?   Yes ❑   No ❑
   If no, where did you purchase this book?_____

   _____

3. How would you rate, on a scale from 1 (poor) to 5 (superior), the cover design?_____

4. On a scale from 1 (poor) to 10 (superior), please rate the following elements.

   _____ Heroine   _____ Plot

   _____ Hero   _____ Inspirational theme

   _____ Setting   _____ Secondary characters

5. These characters were special because_____

_____

_____

6. How has this book inspired your life?_____

_____

_____

7. What settings would you like to see covered in future
   Heartsong Presents books?_____

_____

_____

8. What are some inspirational themes you would like to see
   treated in future books?_____

_____

_____

9. Would you be interested in reading other **Heartsong
   Presents** titles?   Yes ❑   No ❑

10. Please check your age range:
    ❑ Under 18   ❑ 18-24   ❑ 25-34
    ❑ 35-45   ❑ 46-55   ❑ Over 55

Name _____

Occupation _____

Address _____

City _____ State _____ Zip _____

Email _____

NEW MEXICO
Sunrise

Join the Lucas, Monroe, and Dawson
families as they stake their claim to the
"Land of Enchantment." Their strug-
gles and triumphs blend into the
sandstone mesas and sweeping sage
plains of New Mexico, and their
tracks are still visible along the
deeply rutted Santa Fe Trail and the
chiseled railways they traveled. Award-winning
author Tracie Peterson brings their stories to life.

Love and faith in God will conquer any adversity. This
enchanting collection combines four complete novels of
inspiring love that you'll cherish.

paperback, 480 pages, 5 ³⁄₁₆" x 8"

·····Presents·····

Great Inspirational Romance at a Great Price!

Heartsong Presents books are inspirational romances in contemporary and historical settings, designed to give you an enjoyable, spirit-lifting reading experience. You can choose wonderfully written titles from some of today's best authors like Peggy Darty, Sally Laity, Tracie Peterson, Colleen L. Reece, Lauraine Snelling, and many others.

When ordering quantities less than twelve, above titles are $2.95 each.
Not all titles may be available at time of order.

Hearts❤ng Presents
Love Stories Are Rated G!

That's for godly, gratifying, and of course, great! If you love a thrilling love story but don't appreciate the sordidness of some popular paperback romances, **Heartsong Presents** is for you. In fact, **Heartsong Presents** is the *only inspirational romance book club* featuring love stories where Christian faith is the primary ingredient in a marriage relationship.

Sign up today to receive your first set of four never before published Christian romances. Send no money now; you will receive a bill with the first shipment. You may cancel at any time without obligation, and if you aren't completely satisfied with any selection, you may return the books for an immediate refund!

Imagine. . .four new romances every four weeks—two historical, two contemporary—with men and women like you who long to meet the one God has chosen as the love of their lives. . . all for the low price of $9.97 postpaid.

To join, simply complete the coupon below and mail to the address provided. **Heartsong Presents** romances are rated G for another reason: They'll arrive *Godspeed!*